Joe Balha[illegible] ...hor
of crime a[illegible]
novelizatio[illegible] ...Martin's
popular, a[illegible] ...sion.

Also in THE SWEENEY series:

THE SWEENEY
REGAN AND THE MANHATTAN FILE
REGAN AND THE DEAL OF THE CENTURY
REGAN AND THE LEBANESE SHIPMENT

Joe Balham

The Sweeney No. 5: Regan and the Human Pipeline

Futura Publications Limited
A Contact Book

A Contact Book
First published in Great Britain in 1977
by Futura Publications Limited in
association with Arthur Barker Limited.

ISBN 0 8600 7497 8

Printed in Great Britain by
Cox & Wyman Ltd,
London, Reading and Fakenham

Futura Publications Limited
110 Warner Road, Camberwell
London SE5

Three solemn faces, three solemn men, sitting round a bare-topped, fag-end burned, trestle table. The air thick with pipe-smoke and the herbal odour of hand-rolled cigarettes. Sunlight pouring through the windows seemed to bleach everything it touched. The man at the end of the table looked at the other two through red-rimmed eyes that had forgotten sleep.

'It's a bloody tragedy,' he said, 'but I can see no alternative.'

The others nodded, solemnly.

The door opened and Jack Roscoe came in, papers in his hand. 'It's down again,' he said, his voice the only cheery sound the room had heard for an hour.

Three nods from around the table. Jack Roscoe gave a bit of a laugh, then was silent. When the man at the end of the table spoke, his voice was heavy with the burden of momentous decisions. 'We're closing the Emsworth Sluice gate,' he said. 'We have no alternative.'

Jack looked around the table. 'All right,' he said, 'you're closing the sluice gate. Cheer up; it's not the end of the world. The three of you look as if you've just uncovered a crime or something!'

They had, but they didn't find that out for three days.

In the three days following the decision to close the Emsworth Sluice gate, the level of the Filton reservoir sank by eleven feet. At ten o'clock on the third day Jack Roscoe, walking round the paved sloping side of the reservoir, watching the ducks, came across a body lying half in, half out of the water. Being a methodical man he left the body untouched, walked to the office of the Chief Water Engineer at the pumping station on the south side of the reservoir and dialled 999. He waited by the side of the road. The first police car arrived within three minutes. He opened the gate into the field which surrounded the reservoir, climbed into the police car and directed them to a spot just above where the body still lay. Within half an hour six vehicles arrived, including a closed black van with unmarked sides.

A piece of baling wire round the waist of the body had also been twisted several times round half of a paving slab. Jack Roscoe noticed that the paving slab was one of those that had been used for paving the sides of the reservoir, a small stack of which still stood at the edge of the field. He also noticed that the baling wire had not even had time to rust and that the face of the dead man, now bloated almost beyond recognition, was that of an Indian or a Pakistani. He could never tell the difference.

Inspector Jack Regan of the Sweeney – Cockney rhyming slang for Sweeney Todd, Flying Squad – was sitting slumped in the viewing theatre seat. His head was throbbing, his mouth felt as if it had been stuffed with sawdust. He had a hacking cough and his eyes were bloodshot; for once these were not the symptoms of a hangover, but of a stinking head cold he had been trying to get rid of for days. The man from the Immigration Department sitting next to him wasn't helping with his pipe full of some aromatic tobacco. The crowded viewing theatre wasn't helping much either. Although the police had rented it complete with projectionist nobody had thought to turn on the air-conditioning, and the small over-filled room was heavy with the odours of rainswept pavements and heavy serge. Regan looked about him in the half light. They were all there. Superintendent Maynon and Detective Chief Inspector Haskins of the Flying Squad. Four unnamed officers from Immigration, all looking like character actors in some television serial playing the parts of Senior Civil Servants, a sprinkling of senior officers from the London Divisions, two detective sergeants from Scotland Yard, his own sergeant, Carter, looking, as Wogan would say on his morning programme, 'bright eyed and bushy tailed'. The film came to an end. Regan had not watched it this third time round; after all, police films of demonstrations in Trafalgar Square taken from the tops of neighbouring buildings with long-focus lenses, lack something of the entertainment value and suspense of a Hitchcock movie. When the film ended the lights were switched to full. The civil servant with the pipe stood up and walked to the front of the viewing theatre. He took the pipe out of his mouth and held it as if it were a conductor's baton. When he spoke his voice was mellifluous as Yorkshire Heather honey.

'Well, there you see the problem, gentlemen,' he said. 'There can be no doubt that the man on the platform at the base of Nelson's Column is the man known to us all as the "Tiger". I'll give you a brief résumé of his history as you leave. Sufficient to say that several of the police forces of Europe including our own are actively looking for him on suspicion of crimes that range from murder through arson to the use of explosive devices. We have to face the fact, gentlemen, no matter how red our faces may be, that the Tiger was able to come into this country and to depart without let or hindrance. Of course, we in Immigration are quite adamant that he cannot have entered via any of the inlets under our direct supervision. No matter how well the man may have disguised himself, I cannot believe he would have been able to penetrate our surveillance. That is why I have asked for the police forces to be present at this impromptu screening. I feel, and I might add our minister concurs with me, that the affair of the "Tiger" is now a matter for you.'

All the eyes in the room turned and were directed at Inspector Jack Regan who, at that moment, slumped in his chair, was trying to free his balls from the tight hold of the middle seam of his trousers. He sat up straight, took out his handkerchief and coughed. It didn't help that a piece of phlegm inadvertently stuck in his throat and he had to yark to shift it.

'We know it's a needle in a haystack, Inspector,' the man from Immigration said. 'but as of now it's your needle and I'm afraid it's your haystack.'

'Thanks a lot,' Regan said. It was all he could think of at that moment.

Jack Roscoe went to see Major Billboe, the owner of a prosperous riding school at Filton and borrowed a docile sixteen hand former hunter inappropriately called Thundering Cloud. He trotted Thundering Cloud around the edges of the Filton Reservoir, which was shaped like a boomerang extending first south and then west. In the course of his ride he found ten brown-skinned corpses, three white-skinned and one light coffee coloured. Each one had baling wire tied round his waist, attached to a section of paving stone.

Jack Regan was sitting in the Detectives' Office of the Flying Squad in the New Scotland Yard building, staring at the stack of paper work that littered his desk. By his right hand he had a box of Kleenex Man-Size Tissues and his wastepaper basket was half filled with the crumpled paperballs. There were ten desks in the room and the walls, lined with cellotex board, carried pinned up photographs of wanted criminals, memoranda from the Superintendent and the DCI, duty rosters, calendars, pages from Sunday Supplements. The far end of the room was not a conventional wall but a solid sheet of perspex. Beyond the perspex an operations room was equipped with multiple two-way radios, network systems, police teleprinters. A number of rollers let into the ceiling could be pulled down to cover the centre of the perspex wall. These roller blinds were made of transparent plastic and carried printed maps so that at any time an area in which the Flying Squad was particularly interested, could be exposed and marked from either side with coloured crayons. Regan got up from behind his desk, and walked to the perspex wall. The ops room constable on duty, a blonde police woman called Sally, looked up at him.

'Put the UK map up,' he said, 'the whole bloody lot.' So debilitating was his head cold that his eyes didn't even gleam when she reached up and grasped the handle to pull down the map. Sergeant Carter came from behind his desk and stood beside Regan; together they surveyed the limitless coastal boundaries of the United Kingdom.

'It's bloody impossible,' Regan said. 'When you think of the hundreds of small boats that leave these shores every day; when you think of all the fishermen who go out, stay out overnight and then come back in. Any one of them could have nipped over to France and brought back a case of brandy, a Paki, the Tiger.'

'What about all the light aeroplanes,' Carter said. 'You can rent one for ten quid an hour if you have a pilot's licence.'

Regan turned from the map and walked dispiritedly back to his desk. When Sergeant Hilliard saw him sit down he gathered up the papers on which he had been working and brought them to Regan. Regan looked at them, turned them over one by one as his eyes scanned them.

'Yes, that's very good,' he said. 'If we happen to have five thousand men to spare and a couple of years.'

Hilliard's list included checks on all the small club airfields, interviews with the army of full and part time coastguards, interviews with all known informants in all the dock areas of all the ports. It was a thorough business like theoretical exercise, a school essay, but totally impractical.

'Here's what you do,' Regan said. 'One of the men on that plinth at the bottom of Nelson's Column was Alfred Hardecker. I've known him for a long time. Alf's a fixer. He's getting a bit old now, but he's always been on the fringes of these so called spontaneous political breakaway groups. He had his training with the Fascists. Then he swung right over. He was one of the fixers of the Ban the Bomb marches. He's cropped up once or twice outside some of these car factories. Alf has a nice little thing going. He's a professional organizer of agitations. He makes a bloody good living at it too. I want the two of you to go and see Alf. If anybody knows how the Tiger got there it'll be Alf. I wouldn't be surprised to find he was the one who organized it. I want the two of you to have a little talk with him. Nothing official, you understand, and nothing you need make a report about.'

Carter's eyes had narrowed. He knew what Regan was saying. 'You ah, wouldn't want to give us a written memo about that, would you, guvnor?'

'No, I bloody well wouldn't.'

'You weren't thinking of going yourself, were you?'

'What, and give him my germs . . .'

When the two sergeants had gone Regan held the cup that had contained canteen tea below the level of his desk and poured a generous measure of whisky from the half bottle in his bottom drawer. He fumbled in his pocket and drew out the packet of aspirins he'd bought on his way in, swallowed a couple and took a deep draught of the whisky. He looked at the clock on the wall. The time was approaching twelve. Should he try to clear some of the paperwork or go back to his flat in Hammersmith and write the day off? DCI Haskins made up his mind for him when he came into the office. He stood in front of Regan's desk, picked up the cup and sniffed.

'You're starting a bit early these days, aren't you, Jack,' he said.

'I'm trying to chase away this bloody awful cold.' Regan took his handkerchief from his pocket, turned his head and trumpeted into it. When he turned round Haskins was wearing an evil smile he knew so well. 'All right,' he said, 'what have you got for me this time?'

'Well, it seems to me there's only one way to cure a cold like that. You want to get out of London, into the fresh clean country air. The Commander's had a request for help from Bletchley. He's passed it on to the Super, the Super's passed it on to me and I'm going to pass it on to you. Just the job for a man with a cold. Multiple murder, on the edge of a reservoir. They tell me the morgue at Bletchley is a nice warm cheery sort of place, just the place for a man with a cold.'

'Bloody hell. What time tomorrow?'

'Tomorrow? I told them you'd be there at half past one, today! Chief Superintendent Mackenzie's got all the dope. I should watch him though; they say there's only one thing he hates worse than criminals, and that's London coppers trespassing on his patch.'

'But he's asked for us . . .?'

'I'm afraid he hasn't. *He* said he could cope, but the Chief Constable didn't agree with him. It might get a bit hairy.'

'Thanks a bloody lot.'

'That's all right.'

'Why pick me, for Chrissake. Anyway, I was thinking of going sick.'

'But you haven't, have you? That was your mistake. Don't make another by arriving late in Bletchley, will you?'

Detective Superintendent Hamish Dougal Mackenzie was six foot three tall with large bushy eyebrows that bristled over eyes as piercing as dirks. He would have looked better in a kilt with a telegraph pole between his hands. When Regan arrived in his office Mackenzie glowered at him as if he had just crawled out from beneath a stone. His opening words were not encouraging.

'Who and what the devil might *you* be?' he growled. 'Don't try to tell me you're a police officer.'

Regan felt a dribble running down the inside of each nostril, felt them gather into a drop at the end of his nose. He lifted his arm and wiped it away with his sleeve. 'Inspector Jack Regan of the Flying Squad at your service, sir,' he said.

Mackenzie gave a snort and a guffaw. 'Don't make me laugh,' he said, 'or I might blow you away.'

Regan drew himself to his full five feet ten. 'Begging your pardon, sir,' he said, 'but Bletchley and this police station so far as I am concerned, is a tub of shit and you, sir, with due deference, appear to be about the biggest turd in it! Now let's cut out the fucking crap and get on with a bit of police work. Believe me, I'm in no mood for any of your haggis-bashing witticisms.'

Mackenzie brought a hand like a ham down on his desk and roared with laughter. 'Good for you, Regan,' he said. 'I like that. You look like something out of a laundry bag in a Glasgow Geriatric Hospital, but you've got guts, and you're going to need them.'

Five minutes later, after a hair-raising drive which shattered every nerve left in Regan's body, they arrived at the morgue. It was not warm, it was not cosy. Trestle tables had been set up along its length with only two feet between them. On the tables, covered in white sheets, were the bodies of the murdered men. A tall, thin young man wearing a blue and white striped butcher's apron over a once white smock was bending over the figure at the far end of the line, the stench of formaldehyde was so strong that by the time Regan reached the far end of the morgue his nasal passages were completely clear for the first time in days, as if he'd sprayed them with a decongestant. Not recognizing the man with Mackenzie, the pathologist had drawn the cloth over the corpse as they approached. Mackenzie introduced them.

'Dr Furness,' he said, 'this is Inspector Regan of the London Flying Squad. He's come to teach us how to do our job.'

Dr Furness's eyes gleamed with a smile and he chuckled. 'Don't worry, Inspector,' he said, 'Dougal Mackenzie has more wind in him than the bagpipes.' He flicked the cover back from the body. 'We're lucky,' he said. 'I estimate they'd only been in the water for three to four days at the most. That reservoir is a new one and doesn't have too much animal life in it yet.'

'Are they all Pakis?' Regan asked quickly.

'No, they're not. I would say that three of them are European, one is from the Middle East, but the rest are Pakis.'

'Have you formed any conclusions yet? Not for the record. I know we'll get that with the written report.'

'I can see you've had a London education. These provincials think we do it all by magic, think we can look at a body for five minutes and tell 'em all about it.'

'Cheeky bugger!' Mackenzie growled.

'You're one of the worst, Chief.' He turned to Regan. 'Do you want to take notes?' he asked.

Regan shook his head. 'Even I can't read my handwriting,' he said. 'Just tell me what you've got so far.'

'The Pakis were illegal immigrants.'

'How the hell do you know that?' Mackenzie asked.

'Contents of the stomach,' Regan said. 'Condition of the muscles, very little fat. Where they came from they'd be living off rice and maize and not very much of that. Is that right. doctor?'

The doctor was looking approvingly at him. 'I can see you know your stuff,' he said. 'Anything else?'

Regan walked to the bottom of the table and lifted the sheet from the man's legs. 'Look at the condition of the soles of his feet,' he said. 'He hasn't been wearing shoes for very long. Poor bleeder was already getting his first corn. The fruits of civilization.' He pulled the sheet down again. 'What about the Europeans?' he said. 'North or South?'

'One definitely Nordic. One middle, I should say. One definitely Mediterranean. Could be an Italian, could be a Spaniard.'

'And the man from the Middle East . . .?'

The doctor shrugged.

'Impossible to say. I'll make one guess. One of his ancestors was Abraham.'

'That makes him Israeli or Arab. Has he been circumcised?'

'Yes. It wasn't a very good job of work, though.'

'That's a help.'

'In what way?'

'The Israelis take care of that, don't they?'

'So do the Arabs.'

'What? In a little Arab village? Way to hell and gone, chickens and goats, fleas and lice running everywhere.'

'You've got a point,' Furness said. 'I ran paraffin tests on his fingers. The immersion in the water didn't help, but I got a positive reaction.'

It had become a game between the two of them, a private game from which Mackenzie was excluded, and knew it. Regan guessed Doctor Furness had suffered Mackenzie's brow-beat-ing manner in the past and was now enjoying a private revenge.

'He's been handling explosives . . .?'

'Right. He's also been caught, I would say. Lost half his little finger on the right hand, plus part of his cheek and ear.'

'Anything common to all of them . . .?' Regan asked.

'Yes. All were dead when they were put into the water. I would guess the cause of death was asphyxiation. Several of them have traces of aluminium under their fingernails, several have broken fingernails . . .'

This was easy – even Mackenzie could get that one. 'They were in aluminium boxes, without air. They choked to death when the air went out. But first of all, they tried to get out of the aluminium boxes.'

'Full marks,' Furness said. 'You're getting there, Chief!'

Carter came on the telephone. 'No need to shout,' Regan said, 'I can hear you perfectly well. Bletchley isn't the other end of the world you know!'

'We went to see Alf Hardecker. Right slimy one, he is. He said the Tiger was offered to him as a platform speaker. He didn't use him to speak, only to be there, to show by his presence just how futile and contemptuous were the so-called Forces of the Law.'

'At which I hope you thumped him . . .?'

'He turned round suddenly, hit his eye on Hilliard's elbow.'

'I hope Hilliard apologized. You said, "Offered to him". Who did the offering?'

'A voice on the telephone. An Irishman.'

'You don't say.'

'All expenses paid. Plain van to bring the Tiger and take him away.'

'And only a voice on the phone, eh? No names no pack drill.'

'I've just had a call from Interpol. There was a bank job in Bremen this morning. They grabbed the manager on his way in. Killed two of the clerks, and got away with half a million deutschmarks. The manager identified the Tiger from a photograph.'

'Busy little bastard, isn't he?'

'What do we do now. Start on the docks . . .?'

'No, both of you get up here as fast as you can. The Tiger can look after himself for a day or two.'

Jack Roscoe was waiting for them on the roadway that ran parallel with the outer edge of the boomerang of the Filton Reservoir. This time Regan had insisted on Len driving them in the Jaguar that had brought them from London. The car didn't look much, but under Len's tuning in the garage and his capable hands on the driving wheel it had a Formula I acceleration that left even Mackenzie breathless. Roscoe took them down the side of the stakes that had been driven into the grass forming an alleyway about twenty feet wide tied together with white tape. 'We haven't found any significant footprints,' Mackenzie explained. 'There's been no rain and this ground's hard as concrete.'

Regan eyed the grass. 'Yes,' he said, 'and I can see you had a herd of camels milling about before somebody thought to put down the stakes.'

'Hell, Inspector, you know what it's like,' Mackenzie said. 'I was at the other end of the county. Took me thirty-five minutes to get here. Would you believe it, somebody had even driven a car over the grass.'

Regan knew the problem. The police regulations entitled 'Conduct at the Scene of the Crime' don't mean a thing to the average uniformed copper. He turned to Jack Roscoe. 'Right, what can you tell me.'

'I've made a statement.'

'I know you have, but not to me. I'm one of the old school. I like it verbal.'

Jack Roscoe looked across the water. 'Well, it's hard to know what to say,' he said. 'We closed the sluice gate on the Friday night at midnight; the water started sinking, of course. I walked around here on the Tuesday morning first thing just to see how it was doing and saw the body.'

'That sluice gate, it's normally left open. Right?'

'Right. We use it to control the flow of water, to keep this reservoir at the same height, to within an inch or two.'

'Can you show me where the water level is normally.'

Jack Roscoe pointed to a spot half-way up the top paving-stone. 'That's why we only paved this far,' he said. Regan examined the slope of the paving-stones, an angle of about thirty degrees. 'You don't feel like going for a swim?' he said to Roscoe.

'A swim?'

'With your clothes on.'

'A swim, with his clothes on?' Mackenzie said, parroting Roscoe.

Regan turned and shouted to Len who was standing beside the car. 'Break one of those paving-stones in half, Len,' he said, 'and bring it down here.' Len heaved one of the paving-stones from the pile by the edge of the road, picked it up and dropped it back on the pile of stones. It broke into three pieces. 'That's all right,' Regan shouted. Len staggered towards them with a piece of stone held in his hands. He was going to put it down but Regan said 'Hang on to it.' He then put himself in front of Len, jumped up and hung over Len's shoulder, his head dangling down the back, his feet resting against the paving-stone. Len staggered. 'Bloody hell, guvnor,' he said, 'what are you trying to do to me?'

'Right Len,' Regan said, 'throw me into the reservoir.'

Len's face was scarlet. 'Throw you into the reservoir, guv,' he said. 'I can hardly bloody carry you, let alone throw you.'

Regan slid down and stood on his feet. 'You can put the stone down now,' he said. He turned to Mackenzie.

'On the night those bodies were dumped into the water,' he said, 'the water was up to the edge of this reservoir. Whoever dumped them couldn't have known, according to Mr Roscoe's written report, that the sluice gates were going to be closed and the level of the water would go down. Somehow, these bodies went twenty or more feet from the edge of the reservoir. Now, Len's no weakling, and I don't weigh too much but you see he couldn't have chucked me and the paving-stone two feet let alone twenty.'

Jack Roscoe had emptied his pockets into a pile. He walked to the edge of the water. 'How do you want me?' he asked.

'Lying down, flat on your back.' Roscoe did as he was told. 'Right, Chief,' Regan said, 'you and me, two villains. Here's a dead man we've carried to the edge of the reservoir. We've wired a stone on to him and now we want to get him in the water, out of sight. How do we do it?'

'I guess you take his legs and I take his shoulders and we swing him and we throw him in.'

'All right, let's have a go.' Between the two of them they picked up the body of Roscoe, swung him three times and let go. Roscoe's body described a neat arch and splashed into the water eight feet from the edge.

'See what I mean,' Regan said. 'We'd have to be a couple of giants to chuck him twenty feet, especially with a paving-stone on him.'

'I still don't get the point,' Mackenzie said.

'I didn't think you would,' Regan said. He turned to Roscoe standing there dripping water, 'You're not cold, are you?' he asked.

Roscoe grinned. 'You'd be surprised how many times a water engineer falls into the water with his clothes on,' he said. 'What do you want me to do now?'

'Lie down again on your face.' Regan took the stone and put it in the small of Jack Roscoe's back, where it balanced. 'Now Jack,' he said, 'I want you to keep absolutely still. Don't try and do any swimming.' Regan took off his handmade Italian shoes and his socks, rolled his trouser legs up to the knees, grasped Roscoe's legs and eased him into the water. 'Right Jack,' he said, 'Breathe in and hold it as long as you can.' Jack Roscoe did as he was told, Regan lifted his shoulders and dragged them into the water, then he stood up the bank from Roscoe's inert body and pushed. Roscoe's body floated gently away from the side under the buoyancy of the air trapped in his clothing and his lungs. Jack floated at least twenty feet before the air was exhausted and the weight of the stone carried the body below the surface. When Roscoe came up he trod water. 'How deep is it there?' Regan shouted.

Roscoe jack-knifed and went down, obviously a good swimmer. When he came back up again he said. 'Make a guess, Inspector.'

'Eleven-twelve feet,' Regan said. 'You can come out now.'

Mackenzie was looking puzzled. 'I don't see what that proves, Inspector,' he said.

Regan sighed and shook his head. 'Look,' he said, 'those bodies are too near and yet too far. If the villains had used a boat they'd have taken them further out, wouldn't they? If there'd been two of them the bodies would have been nearer in. The point I'm trying to make is, that there was only one villain.'

'And he managed to cope with all of them?'

Roscoe had scrambled back out of the reservoir. 'What's it like around here at night?' Regan asked.

'Quiet, dead quiet. You never get a soul around here. Apart from anything else, we discourage it.'

'I thought not. Right, I'll give you the script. All these men in the back of a lorry. No air. They suffocate to death – God knows how long they've been in the lorry or where they'd come from. The driver of the lorry finds them dead, brings them here, since he knows it's a quiet spot and he won't be disturbed. One by one he floats them out on the water just like I floated Roscoe out, after wiring the paving stones on to them. Then he gets back into this lorry and drives away. So we're looking for one man driving a lorry with aluminium sides.'

Roscoe was looking down at his trousers which were stained with the green slime from the stones at the side of the reservoir. 'Who gets the bill for my trousers?' he said. Regan laughed. 'Send it to Chief Detective Superintendent Mackenzie.'

'You cheeky bugger,' Mackenzie said, 'that'll cost you a drink!'

'I'll tell you one thing, Guv,' Len said when they climbed back into the car, 'you seem to have lost your cold.'

Chief Superintendent Mackenzie had given Regan the use of the office of one of the Superintendents from Bletchley who was away on a course. The windows of the five yards by four yards room looked over an immaculate lawn surrounded by flowerbeds. On an inlaid mahogany table against the wall stood a silver-plate coffee percolator on a lacquered tray with four highly decorated gold-rimmed coffee cups, a silver-plate dish containing multi-coloured sugar crystals, a silver-plate jug containing fresh condensed milk.

Regan picked up one of the cups and turned it over. 'My God, they do themselves proud here in these regions,' he thought, remembering the squalor of the Scotland Yard Flying Squad Detectives' room, the thick, often chipped mug in which his Nescafé was served. He opened the doors of the wall cupboard, saw the bottles of whisky, gin and brandy, the tonic water, ginger ale and soda. He sat behind the desk with its gold embossed green leather top. 'Here's what we do, Len,' he said. 'We'll resign from the Flying Squad, piss off out of The Smoke, get ourselves a cushy number in one of the regions. I'll buy you a trowel and you can take up gardening.'

Len grinned at him. '. . . and join the Golf Club?' he said, eyeing the leather bag on the trolley parked in the corner of the room. 'This is no place for a couple of scruffs like you and me, guvnor,' he said. 'We'd go rotten in a place like this.'

The phone rang and Regan picked it up delicately between his thumb and forefinger, held it to his ear and, in a mock posh voice that caused Len to double up with laughter, said, 'Inspector Regan here!' then had to cover his mouth with his hands to prevent a guffaw. 'Right,' Regan said. 'Ask them if they would be kind enough to step in here.' He put the telephone back on the cradle. The door opened and Sergeants Carter and Hilliard came in. 'Where the hell have you been?' the old Regan said. 'You were supposed to be here hours ago.'

Hilliard had the grace to look sheepish. 'We got lost Inspector,' he said. 'When they said Bletchley I thought they meant Brackley.'

'A right little Cockney you are,' Regan said. 'Anywhere north of Watford is the bloody jungle so far as you're concerned. Right, grab a couple of chairs and come sit over here.' He handed Hilliard a folder of photographs. 'Those are the dead men,' he said. 'You needn't bother about the Pakis. I don't suppose the faces are known. Check that the local boys have got fingerprints.'

'After they've been in the water for three days, guv? They won't be worth much, will they?'

'Don't you know nothing? Didn't they teach you anything about forensics? They peel the finger ends and dry them, shrink 'em down to size. Get those photographs and fingerprints off to Interpol. I want a make on those three Europeans. They didn't get into this country on a package tour. Apart from anything else there are no passports listed among their property. You Carter, can get on your bicycle. Somewhere around here there's a lorry. It's lined with aluminium. Now it could either be an arctic with a container on the back, or it could be a large aluminium packing case. It must be just big enough to hold those men. No, hang on a minute! It could have been bigger! It could have been bigger and three quarters full and they squeezed those men into it. Anyway, check all the local places with lorries that go overseas.'

'No idea which route?'

'None at all. It could be Newcastle to Scandinavia, it could be Immingham to Germany; it could be Felixstowe, it could be Harwich, it could be anywhere around the bloody coast. One thing is certain, the driver knew that reservoir, knew he could be undisturbed there for several hours. So for my money that makes him a local man, working for a local firm.'

'Quite the little Sherlock Holmes, aren't we, guv,' Carter said, looking round at the semi-opulence of the Superintendent's office. 'Next thing we know you'll be wearing a dressing gown and smoking a meerschaum pipe . . .'

'Next thing you know, Sergeant, you'll be pounding a bloody beat in Brixton. Now piss off out of here, both of you.'

The clothing and personal effects of the dead men had been stacked in a room off the mortuary, in trays that looked as if they had been borrowed from a local baker, each carrying a piece of paper on which the numbers 1, 2, 3, etc., had been written. Regan had noticed the brown cardboard tag tied to the big toe of each of the corpses and guessed the numbers would tally. The clothing belonging to the Pakistanis was all cheap cotton, obviously bought in a hot climate and totally unsuitable for England even in the middle of the summer. The shoes in particular were little better than cardboard and, though all were new, all showed signs of wear and distortion. There were no rings, no watches, no wallets, no personal papers of any kind on any of the trays.

'I suppose this is the lot?' Regan said to the constable who had been guarding the collection.

'Yes, Inspector, it looks as if they'd been searched and stripped before being put into the water. It seems to me as if . . .'

'. . . it seems to me as if you talk too much! Just answer the questions. When they want you to do detective work they'll take that uniform off you.' Regan picked up one of the jackets, ran his fingers quickly over it. 'Give us your knife, Len.'

Len produced a pocket knife, opened it, and handed it to Regan, who used it to slash the cheap cotton-shoddy tweed of the inside of the jacket. He put his hand in, there was a ripping sound and he pulled out a flat, black cloth wallet. Inside were four sheets of white paper folded once. When he unfolded them you could read the legend in fine black flowing script. 'I promise to pay the bearer on demand a sum of five pounds.' 'Somebody ought to have told the poor bugger those fivers have been out of date for twenty years,' Regan said, in one of his rare moments of compassion. He felt over each jacket in turn. Each of the Pakis' jackets had something sewn into it somewhere.

One had ten gold wedding rings, one a crudely carved piece of ivory, several had a couple of rupees, one of them an exquisitely inlaid gold pill box of the kind in which the wife of a senior army officer in the British Army of the British Raj would carry her violet scented cachous. Tray number eight carried a different kind of clothing, good cotton underwear, wool socks, brown leather brogues that could have been bought in any of the European capitals, a woollen shirt in a sort of tartan check, a well scuffed but obviously expensive short leather jacket with zipped pockets and a smooth fur collar. The trousers were good corduroy. A hat of a curious design was in the tray; it was made of navy blue felted wool with a peak shorter than the traditional British cap and lined with some hard shiny black material that could have been celluloid or plastic. The rim of the hat was about an inch high and flat. A braided ribbon extended over the peak from left to right. Regan held the cap by the top and turned to the constable, who anticipated his question.

'No fingerprints on that cap, Inspector,' he said.

'Any idea why not?'

'It's not up to me to say, Inspector.' A smile flitted across his face. 'But if I was a detective I'd say they'd have been washed off.'

'Good going.'

The inside pocket of the leather jacket was a skilfully made double pocket. Inside the inner compartment Regan found a grey folder. It was printed in black and bore the words 'Bundesrepublik Deutschland, Federal Republic of Germany'. Beneath the eagle it said 'Personalausweis, Identity card'. The card had eight pages inside and on the third a photograph of a thirty-five-year-old man with no identifying features whatsoever, the sort of face at which you wouldn't look twice in a crowd. On page 2, facing the photograph, was the legend Schirm, Johann. Born 4th of January 1940 in Essen, now having a height of 175cm with blue eyes and no 'unchanging' marks. On page 4 above the identifying stamp of Munich and a signature was the date of issue of the identity card, the ninth of August 1975. On page five the residence of Herr Schirm was given as Munich, 15 Kalbstrasse 70. By the time Regan had finished reading the details the constable, from somewhere no-one saw, had produced a plastic bag which he held out with the neck open.

'I don't think I'll bother,' Regan said, as he slipped the identity card into his back pocket.

Corpse number 9 had been wearing elastic sided boots with one and a quarter-inch platform heels and half inch soles. The uppers had been embossed with a gold stamped pattern. The man had been wearing a lavender coloured shirt, dark blue trousers, a yellow neckerchief, and a three quarter length coat made of a patterned tweed. His long lavender coloured sweater could have been in angora wool, but it was so sodden it was hard to tell. The man's finger- and toenails had been manicured and were lacquered. Regan felt over the jacket and drew a blank. He took the right hand boot, examined it, grunted and twisted the heel. Inside the cavity thus revealed was a bag made of chamois leather. In it were six diamonds each about the size of a lentil. This time when the constable held out his plastic bag Regan dropped the chamois leather bag into it.

'Watch 'em,' he said, 'unless I'm mistaken they're worth ten thousand nicker each.'

Built into the seam of the trousers of the third European was his personal supply of glycerine packets of what looked like heroin.

Of the non-Pakistanis only the man from the Middle East was clean.

It took Len an hour going through London, and Interpol Headquarters in Paris to verify that the Personalausweis with the number he gave them was a phoney. That number had been allocated to a Mrs Inge Mueller of the Kaiser-Wilhelm-Strasse in Munich, who had recently died in childbirth. However, the Interpol computer reading the fingerprints of the man with the Personalausweis had turned up a name; the description fitted Guenther Schiel, a much wanted man suspected of being a founder member of the Baader-Meinhoff gang, a known anarchist, suspected of the assassination of one judge and three members of the Bundesrepublik Judiciary in Bonn. Hilliard reported to Regan that the men from Interpol had sounded very happy on the telephone when he had reported to them that Guenther Schiel had been found dead.

'What about the others?' Regan asked.

'Corpse number 9 is Jacques Laporte, known as The Panther, area of operations Nice, Cannes, Monte Carlo. Cat burglar. Jewel thief. The third man was a Spaniard, Arturo Gomez from Barcelona, leading member of the Basque Revolutionary Council, wanted in Spain, suspected of being on a North European fund-raising mission.

'And the guy from the Middle East?' Regan asked.

'I'll give you two guesses,' Hilliard said.

'What's this, fucking charades. Give me what you've got and be quick about it.'

'PLA. He was one of the guys responsible for the mess at the Munich Olympics, name's Achmed al Mazoor, actually born in Jerusalem.'

'That's better. Nothing on the Pakis, I suppose.'

Hilliard shook his head. 'The computer drew a blank on all their fingerprints.'

'I thought it would.' Regan sat back, dwarfed by the vast leather armchair of the Superintendent, his feet not even touching the ground.

Hilliard and Len stayed quiet; they knew better than to interrupt when Jack Regan went into one of his brown studies. He was not a man who appeared to spend a lot of his time just sitting and thinking. They were more used to spontaneous bursts of action. Regan had learned to play all his cases close to his chest. He was an instinctive, intuitive copper, a hard man who had risen to his present rank by acting fastest and hardest. Hilliard hadn't been with him very long and sometimes suspected he'd been brought in as a foil to Detective Sergeant Carter. A constant running battle was waged between Carter and Regan, a war of badinage and overt jokiness that Hilliard was learning concealed an edge of swordlike sharpness. Len had been with Regan for a good number of years and was the nearest to an intimate and a friend Regan would permit himself, but even he sometimes felt the cutting carborundum edge of Regan's tongue. When Regan spoke his words seemed to be addressed to the elegant flocked wallpaper with which the Superintendent's room had been decorated and which, in Regan's opinion, gave it the atmosphere of the reception room of a French brothel.

'The key to this,' Regan said, 'is not those bloody Pakis. It's those four bloody villains. What we have here is a villain smuggling racket, an underworld pipeline that feeds the shit into and out of this country. I'll bet this is how that bugger the Tiger gets in and out. But where the hell do they come from and where do they come to? That's what we have to find out. A German, a Frenchman, a Spaniard and a bloody Arab and the only thing they have in common is that they're all villains. Three of them are terrorists, but one of them is a poofy French Raffles. It's a hell of a long way from the Basque Separatists, the Baader-Meinhoff Gang and the PLA to the scented bedrooms of the stinking rich of the Riviera. Whenever did you see a revolutionary with lacquered toenails.'

'Never, guv,' Hilliard said, too quickly. Regan glared at him as if to say, 'who the hell was talking to you?' He picked up the telephone and this time when he spoke there was none of the voice affectation he had used previously. 'There is a man called Soames,' he said, 'Inspector Soames of the Special Branch. I don't know his number but get him on the phone. And don't take all bloody day.'

If Mark Tooley was anxious, he tried his best not to show it. Seamus O'Brien was on the telephone, talking to the police headquarters in Bletchley. 'You don't say,' he murmured in that soft Southern Irish accent, 'you don't say. Well, my lad, thank you very much. I'm much obliged to you. There'll be the usual, waiting for you in the garage.'

He put the telephone down, and now his voice was soft as nickel steel, quenched in cyanide. 'That call has just cost me twenty-five quid,' he said. 'Twenty-five quid, just to find out what the police are doing about your bloody cock-up. 'Tis a good job I have friends in high places. You wouldn't happen to know, would you, that they've just called in the Flying Squad out of London. And all because of your bloody stupidity. I don't know what you're using for brains these days, Tooley. I give you a nice easy job that pays silver in your hand, and you go and cock it up. I just don't know what to do with you, Tooley.'

'How was I to know they were going to drain the bleeding reservoir?' Tooley asked, aggrieved. All the world was against him, his attitude seemed to say.

'The mistake you made, Tooley, was to take matters into your own hands. Why didn't you come to me, tell me your passengers were stiffs because you got pissed and forgot to let them out in time. I don't pay you to stop in every wayside pub, swilling down the whisky . . .'

'I was trying to stop a cold . . .'

'Stop a cold! Do you have any idea how much that cold cure is costing me? Apart from what it's costing you.'

'So I don't get my money? £200 a head, that's what I was supposed to get. Don't forget, it was me taking all the risks, driving that bloody lorry through the Customs. And the Immigration. If I was to tell anybody what I know . . .'

Seamus O'Brien was a big man with muscles like hocks of ham, but he came round the chair like a ferret, grabbed Tooley round his throat and ran him, gagging against the wall. 'Don't tell me about talking,' he said, his voice not even strained though Tooley's eyes were almost popping out of his head and his features were turning purple. 'Don't even use the word, talking, to me. There's only one thing I hate more than an Englishman and that's a snout.' His arm moved only twelve inches but Tooley felt the blow explode in his solar plexus, driving the air from him, lining his throat with acid bile. Seamus took his hand away, and Tooley collapsed, gagging.

'Mention that word again,' Seamus whispered, 'and you'll never take another glass of whisky over those lips of yours! Now get out.'

Tooley could hardly move. Seamus picked him up like a bag of feathers, despite his weight, ran him across the wooden shed office, opened the door and threw him into the yard of the farmhouse.

He slammed the door shut. Went back to the ramshackle desk, picked up the telephone. A voice came immediately on the line – they knew better than to keep him waiting. 'Tooley's on his way down,' he said. 'I think he'd better go in the crusher.'

'Right, Seamus. I'll see to that.'

The farm was attached to a gravel pit and a stone quarry. The crusher ate stones of any size, reduced them with large steel balls inside a rotating drum into neat two-inch chunks used for road-work. A few pieces of bone would never be noticed, and the running water would wash away any blood. Mark Tooley wasn't the first man in there and doubtless wouldn't be the last.

Sam Little was driving the Saviem Arctic along the M2, making good time. He'd switched the radio to the BBC, Radio 2, when he'd left Dover. God, it was good to hear a British programme after all that Continental jabbering he'd had to suffer all the way to Iran and back. Still, it was a good life. In four weeks away from home, him and Fred could make seven hundred and fifty each, nearly two hundred quid a week each for delivering a lorry and a trailer load of electronic gear, fridges, tape recorders, pottery, sometimes even sweets and chocolates when they had the refrigerated arctic, from the depot outside Bletchley to the depot in Iran. It was a bloody long haul, but now the company had it to a fine art, with agents at every customs post to speed them through, telexed manifests and customs declarations, the many payments that had to be made, some legal, some backhanded, to the customs people. The Booth Family was a good firm to work for, marvellously organized, with spanking new equipment well maintained. What other firm gave the driver a full set of spares for everything, a complete set of new tyres on the roof, an air-conditioned cab with radio, tapes, a little cooking stove and a comfortable bunk. And what other firm would be willing to take on a driver like Sam, with two strikes against him and the next time he was in trouble, his HGV licence taken away! Well, Sam had straightened himself out, now that he was working for a good employer who'd taken a bit of trouble to be kind to him. Of course, Pat Booth had warned him – any more offences, lose your licence, and your job goes with it. There was a difference between being soft and being understanding. Pat Booth had made no bones about it – lose your licence and you pick up your cards. And Sam Little had got the message, and determined to go straight. It was a bloody good feeling.

The turn-off was coming, where he'd drop his co-driver, Joe, who was going to spend the week-end with his sister. Pat Booth had given his okay. Sam drove the Saviem off the motorway, stopped in the lay-by at the side of the road. Joe's sister was already waiting in her Mini.

'Right-oh,' Sam said, 'see you in a week.'

He waited until the mini had pulled away, then drove the lorry to the roundabout and headed back on to the motorway. He'd driven about twenty miles when the police car overtook him, and flagged him into the lay-by about half a mile further on. Sam pulled on the brake, switched off the engine. God, it was bloody good to have no fear of the police, after all this time. Probably a spot check. Well, the papers were all right. He'd only been at the wheel for three hours out of his allowed total of eleven. The arctic and the trailer were both empty. He had one carton of cigarettes, and one bottle of duty free whisky, well under his allowance. And nothing else on board. He opened the door of the cab and jumped down, stretching his limbs on the tarmac. The first constable came across to him. Without speaking, Sam held out his wallet of papers. The other policeman was going round the vehicle, no doubt looking at tyres. Sam wasn't worried.

The first policeman looked at the papers. 'Don't you have an indicator on this vehicle?' he asked.

'Indicator? Course I have. And it's working. We checked it at Dover.'

'Then why didn't you use it when you pulled on to the motorway?'

Sam thought for a moment. Hadn't he used his indicator? He seemed to remember that he had done. 'I did use it,' he said.

'If you did, we didn't see it, and we were right behind you. You cut in very sudden. If we hadn't been alert you'd have hit us.'

Sam stared at him. 'You what? When I pulled on to the motorway, the carriageway was empty behind me for at least a mile. There was one car in the middle lane, about a quarter of a mile in front . . .'

'Are you calling me a liar, son?' the policeman said, his voice dangerously quiet. Sam felt his face suddenly flush red, and was aware of the other policeman standing behind him. His old feeling of fear returned. 'No, Constable, I'm not calling you a liar,' he said.

The policeman walked to the car, came back holding an apparatus in his hand. 'You know what this is, I suppose?' he asked.

'Yes, it's a breathalyser.'

'Have you any objections to blowing into it for me? If you prefer, you can refuse, of course, and that fact will be noted.'

'I've no objections,' Sam said, relief flooding him. He hadn't had a single drink on board the boat, not a single drink since he set out. He'd filled a flask with tea at Dover, and had taken a drink of that about half an hour ago, but no alcohol, none at all. He almost jerked the bag from the policeman, put the tube in his mouth and blew vigorously. Then he handed the bag back to the Constable.

The second Constable had come round to the front. The first one held the bag up to him. 'You can see that, Constable Laker?' he asked, his voice grim.

Sam could see it. No need to be told. Positive. Bloody-well positive.

'I shall have to ask you . . .'

A black Zephyr came screaming into the lay-by and stopped with a squeal of brakes. A man dashed out of it, rushed to the policemen. 'Big pile-up,' he said, 'about a mile and a half back there. At least six cars and a motorbike. Blood all over the road.'

'You stay here,' the first policeman said to Sam Little. They got into the police car, turned on the flashing light and the siren, pulled on to the motorway and raced up to a gap in the fence about a hundred and fifty yards away, then screamed round on to the other motorway and dashed down the fast lane.

The man from the Zephyr came up to Sam Little.

'Were you having a bit of trouble with the boys . . .?'

'Trouble. You don't know the half,' Sam said dispiritedly. 'I've got two against me, and now I've done a positive breathalyser, even though I haven't had a drink for twenty-four hours. That's my fucking licence gone, for sure, and my job.'

'I don't know so much about that. Maybe I can help. I've one or two friends in high places hereabouts. Maybe you and I can work something out between us, just the two of us. My name, by the way, is Seamus O'Brien.'

Carter put the sheet of paper on the desk in front of Jack Regan. 'I drew a twenty-five-mile ring round Bletchley, guvnor,' he said.

'Why twenty-five?'

'I had to start somewhere. If we draw a blank we can stretch it to fifty miles and start again.'

'*You* can start again! We're not running a bloody cooperative.' Regan had to admit that in the short time at his disposal Carter had done a good job, though nothing would have let him say so to the sergeant. Praise to Regan was something you saved up for a rainy day. Carter had listed the transport firms within the circle with the number of employees, the number of lorries, the number of years in business, the type of goods carried. 'I would have thought there would be a lot more,' Regan said, 'a lot more with a lorry of the kind we're looking for.'

Carter had a smug smile on his face. 'There are, guvnor,' he said, 'but I went to see the Transport Insurance Company in Bedford. They have all the business for these heavy goods lorries and, what's more, they have a computer.'

'And you asked the computer how many firms had lorries with an overseas insurance?'

Carter looked crestfallen. He thought he'd earned kudos for his bright thinking. 'I had a hundred on the list before I went to Bedford. Now there are only three.'

Regan was shaking his head. 'Do you know why you're still a sergeant and I'm an inspector?' It was a rhetorical question and Carter knew better than to reply. 'Because you make assumptions and I don't, that's why! Just because the Pakis and the villains came from overseas that doesn't mean the lorry went overseas. The Pakis could have been dropped by bloody parachutes and then put in the lorry. They could have been brought by submarine and then put in the lorry. Bloody hell, they could have been floated ashore on lilos and then put in a lorry. The only safe assumption to make is that they were suffocated inside an aluminium structure. It could have been a coffin lining. Have you checked the undertakers? They could have been aluminium containers of Italian salami. Have you checked the food importers? They could have been aluminium containers carrying girls knickers from Poland – no, forget that or you'll take it as an excuse to go round lifting skirts. Anyway, this miserable bloody list of three will give us somewhere to start. You take the top one, Universal Transport Limited; give Hilliard the second one 'Rush Freight'. This third one sounds the one for me. A nice family firm. 'Jas Booth & Sons Limited'. They've been in business long enough for the boss's secretary to have learned how to make a decent cup of tea and I could do with a drink.'

The firm of Jas Booth & Sons Limited occupied an old house in the centre of a two acre complex, mostly covered with long low loading sheds. The lorry park itself occupied about an acre with plenty of room for the lorries to turn and back up to the floor height loading platforms. The yard contained a number of new looking forklift trucks and a couple of small mobile cranes. Several containers had been parked on the platforms and were being filled from inside the warehouse by men using wheelbarrows, power trucks, sliding roller ramps which could be angled to discharge deep into the backend of the containers. A dozen or more large lorries were parked along one side, a half a dozen cabs for articulated vehicles, a couple of dozen trailers. The whole depot had a busy, bustling air with many men visible, all working purposefully. Regan noted the high towers with floodlights on them that would permit the work to continue night and day, saw also the cleanliness of the yard, the neat repair shops at one end, the maintenance bays. Len parked the Jag in the small space outside the front of the house next to a Vauxhall Avenger, a Cortina, and a Mini. He went in the front door. The entrance hall was panelled in dark wood and directly in front of him a silver-haired lady with a blue rinse job and tortoise-shell spectacles, wearing an ochre-coloured Jaeger type twinset and pearls, was hitting an old manual Olivetti typewriter as if it had been a naughty boy. Two doors to the left, one door to the right. Staircase leading upstairs with a heavy oak banister. Old oil paintings on the wall. Regan guessed the first one, near the bottom of the stairs, with mutton chop whiskers would be Jas Booth himself. On the left-hand wall were old Sepia tinted photographs. The first one showed a team of six shire horses pulling a wagon which was piled impossibly high with barrels.

'From these humble beginnings . . .' Regan murmured.

'I beg your pardon,' blue rinse said. 'Can I help you?' Regan took out his ID card. She was the type to need identification. He'd seen a similar set of faces on drawings of the ladies knitting around the base of the Bastille. She read the card as if it were a page of the Bible, held it at arm's length to compare the photograph with the reality. 'If you looked like your photograph, Inspector,' she said, 'I would have told you you ought not to be at work today. Now what can I do for you?'

'Used to work for Jas Booth, did you?' Regan said, 'though I don't suppose he's around any more. Could I see his great grandson or whoever is running the business these days.'

Blue rinse grinned at him. 'Touché,' she said. 'His name is Mr Pat and he's not the great grandson. He's actually only the nephew.' She cranked a handle on the switchboard, spoke into a telephone that looked as if it had been designed by Edison. Almost immediately the door on the right opened and the space was filled with the bulk of a very large man, dressed in a very heavy tweed suit. The man wore old-fashioned half spectacles low down on his nose; he crinkled his eyes to look over the lenses, then ushered Regan into his office.

'Pat Booth,' he said. 'What can I do for you, Inspector Regan?'

The contrast between this office and the reception hall was amazing. Sitting in a corner was a modern Decca Telecommunications centre manned by two girls, neither over twenty-five. Linked to the radio set-up was a telephone switchboard of the push-button variety.

'That's our little toy,' Pat explained, seeing the direction Regan was looking. 'We need to keep in touch, you know.'

'Looking outside, at the reception desk . . .'

'Miss Pringle has been here a long time,' Pat said. 'She used to work for my Uncle, the founder of the firm. We keep her on; she's good for the image. And all the men love her. She's a regular Mum to all of them, and their wives, too, when they're away. She has a mind like an encyclopaedia, oddly enough about lorries and engines and routes and ferries, all that sort of thing. Of course, it's all different now. We started by carting liquids by horse-drawn trams, as they were called in those days. Now a lot of our business is overland to the Middle East, as well as to all the docks.'

It smelled wrong, didn't it? Regan felt already that he was wasting his time and the time of Pat Booth. Firms as old as this one, as overtly-successful as this one; don't go in for smuggling Pakis at a few hundred a time. It just wasn't worth their while to endanger something that had been built as solidly as this. Regan had been in to plenty of firms which seemed okay on the surface, but had a subcutaneous rot. Firms with cash flow problems that turned bent to balance the budget. But blatantly, this wasn't one of them. Pat Booth was waiting for him to speak, and for the first time in a long while, Regan didn't know where to begin.

'I don't know if you can help me,' he said. 'I'm looking for a driver of a vehicle that goes on to the Continent. A regular run, I imagine.'

Pat Booth was quick. 'You don't look like a customs officer,' he said. 'We get a lot of them coming here. We have an arrangement. A lot of our stuff is sealed at the point of origin and the customs come here and break the seals. One of our warehouses has been made into an in-bond warehouse. It relieves the pressure on the docks and gets our lorries moving faster.'

'No, it's not a customs job.'

'I can tell you this much. We're very strict with all our drivers. When I set them on I read the Riot Act. Any man caught with as much as a bottle of scent in his cab over and above his ration loses his wages, his distance bonus, his allowances and what's more important to him, his job and his good name. The last one we had must be six years ago now, silly bugger was bringing brandy in a jerry can; a customs officer dipped a stick in it and that was it. I reckon it cost the driver the thick end of five hundred pounds and his good name. He's selling pots and pans in Northamptonshire market right now. 'Cause everybody knows that if Jas Booth & Sons fire a man, he's not worth re-employing. There are a lot of fly-by-night firms in this game, Inspector, and one or two good ones. I'd like to think we're among the good ones.'

'But a driver could go bent?'

'There are more things in heaven and earth, Inspector! A driver could go bent. Let's assume that's one of mine. What can I do to help you? It goes without saying you can have the run of the place, bring as many men in as you like. You can have all the books to look at. We've nothing to hide. If it's a matter of a driver, I should start by having a word with Miss Pringle. Like I said, she's as good as a mother to them all.'

'How about your vehicles,' Regan said. 'I suppose they are spread all over the face of the world.'

Pat Booth glanced at a map of Europe that covered a half of one wall. 'As it so happens Inspector,' he said, 'and I can't tell you the last time this has happened – you've come on the one day when all the vehicles are in the yard. The first one goes out tomorrow at midday for Liverpool docks. If it's a vehicle you're interested in, you're in luck.'

'One more question,' Regan said. 'When the vehicles come in presumably somebody checks the inside of them.'

Pat Booth smiled. 'You don't know how we run this business, Inspector. Check is hardly the word. When every vehicle comes in, no matter where it's been or how long it's been out, it's cleaned top to bottom, inside and out. We use steam hosepipes. What's more, the engine is given a check-over that would make an airline maintenance team look like a bunch of boy-scouts. Do you know, we haven't had a breakdown on the road for over two years. That's how this firm has been built, Inspector. You know the first thing my uncle said when I came here to work as a lad of fourteen. "Allus water and oat the 'osses and swill the wagon and tha'll nivver lack for customers".'

The maintenance team were at work on a Saviem Arctic, swarming over it like fleas. From inside the trailer Regan could hear the hiss of steam and the swish of high-powered water. When the noise stopped, two men appeared at the door wearing rubber coveralls, gumboots and hats. The maintenance foreman beckoned them over and introduced Regan.

'I believe you do all the wagons,' Regan said. 'Which one of you is Jim Holden?'

The smaller of the two men nodded his head. 'I am,' he said. 'Usually I work days and Burt here works nights. But with all the wagons in for once we're both in it together.'

'Would you come in this trailer with me,' Regan said. He

climbed up the step and into the trailer which was twenty feet long with flat, clean, aluminium sides. He put his hand up against one of the walls and dragged his nails down, making a thin screech.

'Bloody hell, that puts my teeth on edge,' Jim Holden said.

'Mine too.' Regan went on doing it, pressing harder and harder each time. Soon the marks of his nails were clearly visible as scratches in the soft metal. 'See those marks,' Regan said, 'I'm looking for a trailer like this one – by that I mean lined with unpainted aluminium – which has a lot of scratches like that in it. Have you seen one?'

'Scratches like that? Well, when some of them come back, bloody hell, you wonder what they've been doing. I remember one with a great knife slash all the way along it, just as if somebody stuck a knife and dragged it. But scratches like that . . .?' He turned to Burt. 'Have you seen anything like that, Burt?'

Burt shook his head.

'And you *would* see it?' Regan asked.

'Oh, yes, we'd have to. You see, what happens is this. First of all we use the water hose and wash everything out, then we use the steam and then we come over it with a scrubbing brush, dipped in detergent, and then we use the steam again. We go over every inch of these insides four times. You see we also carry food and the hygiene inspectors are shit hot. I mean they come in here, you see where that panel meets the floor there, well, they scrape that with like a nail file. And that goes into a test tube. If they find any bacteria, it's that truck off the road. You see, a lot of our stuff goes to hot countries. It wouldn't take much for the whole of this trailer to be rotten with germs. And I'll tell you something, it doesn't matter about bloody hygiene inspectors. Our Mr Booth, Mr Pat we call him, he's the toughest of the lot. If he can't see his face in that bloody ali it's a rocket, and I've never ever known him have to tell any man twice. An interview with Mr Pat is worse than being put through a bloody mangle.'

'No scratches.'

'Sorry mate, no scratches. I tell you what, I'll take you round the yard. You find what you're looking for and I'll put your name on my football coupon this week. I've got a bloody certain eight draws.'

'You should be so lucky,' Regan said.

Miss Pringle made a beautiful cup of coffee. 'This desk and telephone are all show,' she said. 'I'm a sort-of unofficial Mum to the drivers and their wives. In a larger organization you'd call me the Welfare Officer, but we don't go in much for titles round here. What did you want to ask me?'

'I don't know . . .'

'Well, that's a good beginning. Obviously, it's something to do with one of the drivers, or Mr Pat wouldn't have suggested you talk to me. Not that you're doing any talking . . .'

'I'm too busy enjoying this coffee of yours. Let me put it this way. Mr Pat, as you call him, is quite convinced that none of your men is what we call "bent".'

'In what way, "bent"?'

'I don't know exactly. It's early days, yet. I've only just begun an investigation into the deaths of a number of men. I have reason to believe those men might, just might, have been brought into this country illegally, in a lorry. That would need a lorry driver.'

'It would need *two* lorry drivers. All our overseas lorries have a crew of two, minimum. Sometimes even three.'

'Right, let's say, two. It's been my experience that a man who's gone bent can't hide that fact from people who know him well, who take an interest in him. When we hear of a bank clerk, for example, taking off with twenty thousand from the till, I blame the manager, who ought to have seen the signs sooner. Mr Pat said you were close to the men. Have you seen any signs, anything at all?'

Miss Pringle thought for a moment. 'These signs, Inspector, I see them every day. If you knew the number of times I've sat a man down with a cup of coffee in his hand and said, "Come on, tell me what's wrong!" It usually turns out to be something in the marriage. Either his wife hasn't been paying the grocery bill when she should, or his kid's failed an examination because he hasn't been studying hard enough. Often an advance against future salary will wipe the frown off his face. We had a case of a man only three weeks ago. Walked about with a long face. Backed a lorry against one of the loading bays and damaged it. He got the full treatment. It turned out his wife wanted a new car and had been nagging him about it. He'd taken a part-time job as an all-night taxi-driver to earn it for her. But he had a guilty conscience. We like our drivers to get a good rest when they come off the job. One of our drivers right now, he's disappeared. He'll be back in a week to pick up his money before he goes out again. I expect he's having a few days holiday at the coast, somewhere. No, I'm afraid I don't think I can help you. We've got a rough and ready crew working here, but they're all good drivers, all reliable. They're not saints – that's not what I mean to say – but if any one of them turns out to be bent, then I'll be very surprised.

Hilliard had drawn a blank. 'The insides of all their lorries are painted,' he said. 'Special paint, anti-rust, anti-germicide.'

Carter had fared no better. 'They have an overseas insurance,' he said, 'but they don't use it. In fact, I think the company's about to go broke. They brought in a young whiz-kid a couple of years ago. He took out the International insurances. Tried to break into the Iran runs. Had a disaster when the brakes failed on one of his lorries and killed ten people in Yugoslavia. The court ruled it was faulty maintenance. Since then, they haven't been able to pick up a single overseas run. Mostly they're carting dirty cargoes round England, work nobody else wants.'

'Could one of the drivers be trying a bit of private enterprise?'

'I wondered that, but the lorries don't have the right plates.'

'Could one of the drivers have his own plates?'

Carter hadn't thought of that one. 'I'll go back and check that one,' he said.

'You'd better. And next time, don't come back with a half-arsed story. If there *is* a pipeline in existence, it'd need a full organization, wouldn't it? And getting plates wouldn't be, shouldn't be too difficult.'

When Carter had gone, Regan went back to the morgue. Dr Furness was at the far end of the room, standing at a bench which contained a row of flasks and beakers. 'I've had to simplify things a bit,' he said. 'I don't have the facilities here for refrigeration in such quantity.' He held up one of the flasks and twirled it around gently, agitating its contents.

'What are you doing, making wine?' Regan said jokingly, and immediately wished he hadn't.

'No, all these are stomach contents,' Dr Furness said. 'We pump out the stomachs, standard procedure.'

Regan turned away from the bench, suddenly gagging.

'We learn a lot that way,' Dr Furness continued, blandly, as if they were discussing a scientific theory. 'One thing is particularly interesting. Two of the men had been drinking. Whatever it was, it hadn't passed through them. Not all the way. We know the chemical composition of most of the beers, but this is a new one. It'll take me a day or two to identify it.'

Regan looked at the row of flasks, and could taste Miss Pringle's coffee again. I'll leave you to it, Dr Furness,' he said. 'Give me a ring when you make any progress.'

Sam Little's wife Maud put down the crossword puzzle she was trying unsuccessfully to complete. 'You'll have to tell me what it is, sooner or later,' she said. 'Why don't you tell me now, and get it over and done with. You've been sitting there all day with a long face. You haven't even switched on the tele for Match of the Day. You don't look as if you've got a temperature, or anything. So what is it?'

'Leave me alone, can't you Maud,' he said grumpily. Not like him at all.

One of the pleasures of him being away so often was that every time he came back it was as if they were starting a new honeymoon. But this time, nothing. She'd even had to have a go at him to get a few kisses out of him. And when they finally did get together in the bed, it was as if he'd become a savage animal, banging away into her without any of the loving gentleness she'd become used to, as if he was using her body to get rid of his frustrations, rather than to share love and tenderness with her. He got up and stood beside her chair, held out his hand and touched the side of her face.

'It's been a good life, hasn't it, since I stopped drinking.'

'Nobody could have wished for a better.'

'This job means a lot to us, doesn't it? It's letting us catch up a bit, after the years of boozing it all away. That's worth something, isn't it?'

'It's worth everything, Sam. You've become a different man since you started getting a bit of something behind you. This house, the furniture, the nice car, a bit in the bank. I think you're a man who needs that, Sam, and I'm very glad you've found a way to get it. Not for me, but for yourself. I hope nothing ever happens to come between you and that job, you and the independence that job gives you.'

He took his hand away. 'You're a bloody Princess,' he said and bent to kiss her. 'I've got to go out for a minute or two. Make a phone call. I'll call at the off-licence on my way back and get a couple of bottles of beer . . .'

'And we'll drink 'em in bed, like we used to . . .'

'Why not . . .?'

There was a lot of clicking on the line when Sam dialled the number Seamus O'Brien had given him and identified himself. They'd instructed him to put the phone down, and had called him back. Sam was too innocent to realize Seamus was taking no chances on a bugged line. Finally he found himself hearing that already familiar Irish voice.

'What can I do for you, Sam? Have they given you a trip?'

'Yes, they have. I leave tomorrow. Innsbruck, not Iran.'

'Sure that's lovely. You'll be back sooner from Innsbruck,

won't you. That pretty wife of yours won't have to wait so long . . .'

'Yes, Mr O'Brien, but . . .'

'Oh, call me Seamus. Everybody does . . .'

'Yes, Seamus, well, I won't be able to do what you asked . . .'

'Won't be able? I'm counting on you, Sam. Those two policemen I've had to bribe to hold off with that breathalyser, they're counting on it, too. You see, what they've done, is they've made out a full report and they've accidentally-like put it into the wrong file. It's all dated and everything. Anytime we let them down, they can accidentally-like find it again, know what I mean? You mustn't let us down, Sam.'

'No, Seamus, I'm not letting you down. But one thing we both forgot. I've got a co-driver, you see. And Joe's as straight as a die. He's also very right wing, a right Enoch-Poweller. Me, I don't mind the Pakis coming in to join their husbands and fathers. I agree with you it's a crying shame to keep families apart – let one in, you've got to let them all in. But Joe won't see it that way. Honest, Seamus, if he even gets a smell of Pakis, he'll blow a gasket.'

There was a brief silence on the line. 'Don't worry,' Seamus said, 'Somehow I don't think Joe will be making this trip with you.'

Pat Booth called Sam Little into his office the following day. Despite Seamus's assurances that the police had been bought off, Sam couldn't help a feeling of apprehension. Was Pat about to fire him? That breathalyser would lose Sam his licence and his job for sure.

'Ah, Sam,' Pat said. 'Everything all right for your trip today?'

'Everything's fine, Mr Pat. I've picked up all the documentation from the Dispatch Office. I've just got to see the cashier about my foreign currency and the travellers' cheques.'

'Right. I'm sorry to send you out again so soon. Mark Tooley was booked for this run but he seems to have gone away somewhere for a few days and left no address at his digs. He'll be back with a hangover – we've still got his money here from the last trip. Just one more thing. How do you get on with Arthur Naylor, Mark's co-driver.'

'All right. I've done a couple of trips with him in the past. We've always got on.'

'Good. You see, your own co-driver, Joe, has just called in to say he's had a bit of an accident. Nothing serious. It seems he got into an argument with a car, and the car won. The hospital says it's a fractured tibia, and he'll be in plaster for a month or so.'

Sam felt his face begin to flush. So this was what Seamus meant when he said, he didn't think Joe would be making the trip. Sam had had no illusions when Seamus had made his first proposal, but he hadn't realized just how ruthless Seamus could be. He'd have to watch himself.

'Arthur and me will be all right together,' he said. 'Anyway, it's only the short run to Innsbruck. Give us a chance to settle down.'

On his way out of the office, Sam stopped at Miss Pringle's desk. 'If you're getting a collection for Joe,' he said, 'put me down for £20.'

'No, that's too much,' Miss Pringle said. 'A pound would do.'

'Twenty,' Sam said, fiercely.

The Managing Director of Walworth's 'Hatters by Appointment to H.R.H. Prince Albert', looked about ninety years old, with a thin, long, bloodless face, hands in which you could see the outline of every vein and bone, wearing a short jacket made of some kind of black cottony material. He rose to his feet when Regan was shown into his office and extended a hand. Regan held it as if it were bone china then sat down in the deep leather armchair.

'What can I do for you?' the managing director said. 'We don't often have the pleasure of talking with policemen here.'

Regan took the hat out of his pocket. The dark blue hat from the corpse number 8. He handed it to the Managing Director, who turned it over in his hands. 'Don't see many of those these days,' he said. 'We once tried to market an English version but somehow it didn't catch on.'

'You know what it is?'

'Oh yes, they're quite common.'

'Since you say, an English version, would I be correct in assuming it is foreign.'

'You would, young man. Oh, I can see you're a detective all right. It's what they call an "Elbsegler". Made for sea captains originally. Very old design, hasn't changed at all.'

'Could you tell me where it comes from?'

'Oh, I'm sorry. Didn't I say? The original design comes from the Hanseatic days. The noble days of sea captains. It was a wonderful age of adventuring and commerce. I should have been alive then.'

'Hanseatic?'

'Ah, yes, the Hanseatic League, and all that. They weren't afraid of a bit of a storm. Mostly under sail, too. Not like today when it's all computers and radar . . .'

'But where, where?'

'Oh, didn't I say? Hamburg, of course, that's where the Elbsegler comes from. Hamburg. The capital of the Hanseatic League . . .'

'And all that . . .'

'That beer,' Dr Furness said on the telephone. 'Do you want to come and see what I've got?'

Regan's stomach heaved at the thought. 'You wouldn't like to tell me over the telephone,' he asked.

'Very well. No wonder we didn't recognize it right away. It's a special beer, brewed and drunk only in May. It's called "Maibock".'

'From Hamburg, Germany?' Regan said.

'I was nosing about this afternoon,' Sergeant Carter said, 'looking for a lead about the plates, and I got a feeling. You know the way sometimes you say you've got a smell of something not right.'

'Usually your socks, Carter. We'll make a copper of you yet.'

Carter, Hilliard, Regan, and Len were crouched in the angle of a shed with a wall, behind a low wooden partition. The top rail of the partition left a gap of about an inch and a half through which they could see the loading yard. They'd been there an hour; Carter had been there since dusk.

'I watched the last driver come out and he locked the gate. There seemed something odd about the way he did it, so when he'd gone, I came and had a look at it. He'd put the padlock on, but hadn't put the hasp through it. Anybody could have opened it. That's when I got the funny feeling.'

Across from where they were hiding, a wooden hut stood with an open door. Beside it, a tractor with a hydraulic shovel on the front. Beside the shed was a heaped pile of what looked like wet sawdust and stank, even from that distance, of manure and stale beer. As they watched, they saw the hordes of rats scuttling around the bottom of the pile, fat, sleak and ugly. One light, on a tower, shone fitfully over the yard, which looked a shambles compared with the yard Regan had seen at Jas Booth.

'What the bloody hell is that stuff?' Regan asked, wrinkling his nose.

'It's some sort of spoil from the brewery. They take it from here to some place near Derby, a chemical factory. Nobody else will carry it. If it wasn't for that, so I was told, this firm would go broke.'

The gate into the yard opened suddenly and an Army jeep came in, driven by a man in Army uniform, wearing a corporal's stripes. The back of the jeep was covered. One man, also in Army uniform, was sitting beside the driver. A third man came through the gate and shut it behind them. The jeep drove to the back of a high sided tipper lorry. When the third man came into the light, Regan saw he was wearing the stripes and crown of a quartermaster sergeant.

Regan whispered to Len, 'Back off and get outside. Find some way to jam that gate shut and then put in a call to Mackenzie. Tell him, no bloody sirens, no flashing lights. If I see or hear any trace of them getting into position, I'll have his knackers.'

The three men didn't speak. One dropped the tail of the tipper lorry, and leaped aboard. The other two reached inside the jeep, took out apparently heavy boxes about twelve inches square and three or more feet long. One by one they slid the boxes into the back of the tipper lorry and stacked them in the centre. There were ten boxes in all.

'You, Hilliard, over there by the gate. You, Carter, behind that heap of shit. When I'm ready, I'll whistle. When you hear me, come out, and be prepared for anything.'

The soldiers finished the loading, and re-fastened the tailgate of the lorry. The quartermaster sergeant went over to the tractor, started it, and used its shovel to load the back of the tipper with muck from the pile. The three of them threw a tarpaulin over the stinking cargo, and tied it down. Then the man who'd been sitting next to the driver of the jeep took off his uniform, revealing civilian trousers and a jacket underneath. He climbed in to the tipper lorry and started its engine. Regan leaped over the low wooden wall.

'Hold it,' he shouted, 'police.'

The two soldiers stood stock still. The driver of the tipper, sensing something was wrong, opened the door of the cab and looked out. Regan walked briskly across the yard. 'Hold it,' he said, 'police. We're all round you, so don't try any fun and games. Not with me!'

The two soldiers looked about them. No signs of anyone else. The driver jumped out of the tipper lorry and the three of them formed an arc. Regan, seeming unconcerned, walked into the middle of the arc.

'I'll say this for you,' the quartermaster sergeant said, 'if you *are* a copper, you've got guts.' The signal between them was imperceptible, but Regan could read danger like a nurse can read a thermometer. He whistled, loud, twice, before the three of them jumped him. Stiff arm in the quartermaster sergeant's Adam's-apple. Too much Naafi living; he gagged and came forward. One man had an arm lock round Regan's shoulders, but Regan smashed his hand down and felt the hard sharp blade jab between the man's legs. Then his head was spinning from a hammer blow on the side of his temple, and he felt a quick gush of blood into his eyes as he went down to his knees. Through the haze he saw Carter with a block of wood in his hands and the driver's skull in front of him. A boot in his middle, impossible to say whose, swing his arm sideways and feel his elbow crack into a kneecap and a hollow snapping sound. Shake his head to try to clear the blood, grunts and heavy breathing and the solid chunky smash of hard fists on flesh. And then, as suddenly as it began, it was over. He lifted his head, found he was half squatting, half kneeling on the ground. Hilliard bent forward with a handkerchief in his hand and wiped Regan's forehead. The cut stung and he flinched, but heard Hilliard say, 'only a flesh wound'. He struggled to his feet. The three men were out cold. Carter was looking at his hand.

'I've got a bloody splinter in here,' he said, 'and it's giving me gyp!' The door of the yard opened.

'Can we come in now?' Chief Superintendent Mackenzie said, 'or is this a private party?'

'You've just had a holiday,' Superintendent Maynon said. 'You took three days off when you went to Calais. It's on your file, isn't it, Chief?'

Haskins thumbed through papers like a squirrel sorting nuts. Paperwork was Haskins' life blood. It was precisely because Regan had a total contempt for the written word that Haskins spent much of his time trying to bring Regan to heel.

'Yes, Superintendent, I have the written application here, countersigned by me and authorized by you.' He smirked with satisfaction. For Detective Chief Inspector Haskins the pen was indeed mightier than the sword.

'It may have escaped your attention,' Regan said, with deliberate slow heavy patience, 'that my so-called holiday got us a helluva lot of heroin, and enough Deutschmarks to affect the balance of bloody payments. And, what's more, while I was supposed to be lolling about on vacation I managed to solve a murder and break up the South London Gang. Anyway, I'm not asking for a vacation. I'm asking for a suspension from duty and the necessary funds to bugger off to Germany to carry out what Mr Haskins in all his literary glory would call a clandestine investigation.'

'Without apparently giving us any details,' Haskins said.

'I can't give you any details. I don't have any. All I have is a good clue, two good clues in fact, that a human pipeline into this country passes through Hamburg. I want to go there and find out, it's as simple as that. But I don't want to go there as a copper. Not officially.'

'And yet you want to take a sergeant with you?'

'That's right,' Regan said.

'And you don't want him suspended from duty?'

'That won't be necessary. I'm not trying to get him into a pipeline, am I?'

'What's happened to that teddy bear of an inspector of yours,' Miss Pringle asked Sergeant Carter. 'He strikes me as a man who needs someone to cuddle him.'

'I'll tell him what you said,' Carter said, grinning.

'You won't, young man. You won't have the nerve. Where is he? I liked it when he came to see me. You look too much like a VAT snooper.'

It was an inauspicious beginning. When Miss Pringle heard what Sergeant Carter wanted, she really hit the roof. 'So, you are a snooper, after all,' she said. 'My instincts never let me down. Look, I told your inspector. Our drivers are all right. If they weren't, I would know it. I don't sit here with my eyes closed,' she said.

Carter couldn't resist it. 'Then how is it you haven't seen that the zip on the side of your dress is unfastened,' he asked. 'I can see your drawers from here!'

'You cheeky young devil.' She twisted round, saw that the

zip was, in fact, down, and that a long stretch of her slip was showing. Though she wouldn't dream of admitting it to the sergeant, she had been getting a little forgetful recently. She even realized that Pat Booth, Mr Pat as she called him, knew it. One by one, all her executive responsibilities had been gently removed from her. She hadn't minded; the firm had taken care of her retirement, whenever she cared to take it, in a most generous way. She really only came here each day for something to do, someone to talk to. Mr Pat had made it quite clear to her that she could continue to come as long as she cared to. Now, it seemed, all she had left was the welfare work she did among the drivers and their families.

'I'm not making any suggestions against any of your drivers,' Carter said. 'Most police work is simply a matter of elimination. All we want is the name and the photograph of every driver with this firm who's scheduled to do a Hamburg run, regardless of ultimate destination. And only during the next month. The name, a photostat of his photograph, the number of the vehicle he will be driving, his destination, his cargo, the date of crossing Harwich to Hamburg each way. That's not so difficult, is it? Then we can say to our chaps, right, that's Fred Bloggs, of Booth's. He's going to Istanbul with a load of machinery, he'll be coming back Tuesday the twelfth empty. Since he's with Booths, and personally vouched for by Miss Pringle, we can forget about him. We need to *eliminate*, don't you see?'

'What about the other companies?'

'They've all agreed to co-operate. I wouldn't think you'd want to stand out against them, would you? I understand Mr Booth is the President of the Federation. It was Mr Booth who told me to speak to you, you know. I'm not some urchin off the street. Mr Booth said, and I quote, "Go to Miss Pringle. She's got everything at her fingertips. If anybody can help you, it's Miss Pringle". He seems to think the world of you ...'

'You've got a silver lining to your tongue, lad. It'll get you into a lot of beds ...'

'What a pity I'm not a bit older,' he said.

She blushed, then gave him a folder she'd already prepared, containing all the information he wanted. Including the photographs of each of the drivers who'd be travelling the Harwich-Hamburg route.

It was raining in Hamburg. The Pension Schmidt was on the Ferdinandstrasse, near the railway station and the lake known as the Binnen Alster. Standing in the window, Regan could look across the street at a fishmonger's shop, next to a Chinese restaurant and a Tchibo coffee shop. The Pension Schmidt had six rooms – Regan had noticed six hooks on the wall when he signed the register – and was run by a large jolly woman who giggled constantly and shook like a jelly, and her tall thin patriarchal husband. Both could have been eighty, both spoke a sort of English and seemed to understand Regan who spoke no German at all.

'Zwei Zimmer? Two rooms? Yes. We give good German breakfast. Bread, jam, cooked egg. Clean house. Very quiet. No, how you say, drunk. Anybody drunk, I give fist and send away. Sign please.'

Regan and Carter signed, produced their passports and went upstairs. The rooms were clean though sparsely furnished. Regan eyed the vast eiderdown on the bed and wondered how the hell he'd be able to keep it on him when he slept. He unpacked the few things he'd brought with him, went again to the window and looked out at the rain. That was one thing he'd forgotten, a raincoat, though he saw that lots of people were wearing plastic macs and rain covers they pulled over the normal headgear. There was a knock on the door and Carter came in.

'What's the plan guv?' he said.

'The plan is that there's no plan. Your job is to stay in the background but near enough that if I want you I can get hold of you quickly. Everywhere I go, everything I do, you shadow me and cover. And if I get into trouble you run like hell for the nearest – what do they call them here? – gendarme?'

'You mean "Schupo".'

'You're the one with the A-level German. Me, I never went to school. I was always too old.'

He looked out of the window again reflectively. Carter would never know how true that was. In primary school in Hammersmith you learned enough to pass the tests and no more. It wasn't an education, merely a few facts you grabbed along the way in order to survive and make sure you moved from class to class each year so that when your time came you could leave at the first possible moment. You learned everything and were taught nothing. Your education began at half past four when you ran out of the big iron gates of the pre-Victorian building as if it was a prison. Your classroom was the backstreets of Hammersmith. Your university the glittering light of Hammersmith Broadway. Passing tests became a habit, even the test to get into the police. Joining the police force was a matter of survival. It was a steady job and gave a pension. You had to serve forty years hard labour but it was there at the end. You went into the police with a hidden anger, without knowing what you were angry at. The whole of society was a villain. Only later did you reluctantly begin to accept that the downtrodden 'us' of your childhood became the villainous 'them' of your maturity. Only later did you realize that your juvenile heroes grew up to be petty crooks, pimples on the arsehole of humanity. That was your education, Hammersmith-style and A-level German was a flight into outer space.

'Right,' Regan said, 'use that education of yours to go over to that shop and get us two cups of coffee.'

'They don't do take-out coffee in Germany,' Carter said smugly.

'That's your problem, lad, isn't it. I'm thirsty, so get cracking.'

The taxi dropped Jack Regan at the side of the Elbe near the boat station for the Prinz-Lines, the ferries that went from Hamburg to Harwich. Across the vast stretch of the river

Regan could see the miles of wharves and jetties, the hundreds of boats of all sizes, some moored discharging cargo, some taking on cargo, some being towed up and down the river with tugs. It was the busiest port he had ever seen. He took the map of Hamburg out of his pocket, walked along the Elbe towards the fish market, located the steps and climbed them, seeing on his right the modern building of the Holsten Brewery with the dark observation windows of the public restaurant on its roof. Yesterday, he and Carter had eaten a meal up there – God knows what the Superintendent would say when he saw the amount of the bill on Regan's expense account.

He studied the map for a few moments, then put it away in his pocket, relying on his visual memory. Straight up the Davidstrasse past the mouth of the Herbertstrasse with its two angled entrances that prevented anyone seeing the brothels it contained and its notices banning women from entering. No doubt the girls who worked there were afraid of the amateur competition. He carried on until he was opposite the police station known as the Davidswache at the junction of the Reeperbahn and the Davidstrasse. He didn't look at the building but turned left and after a few yards crossed the Reeperbahn to the entrance to the Grosse Freiheit, proud of having found it the first time. Down the Grosse Freiheit with its pubs and nightclubs, the busy throng parading up and down going nowhere. Men and women, men who looked like women, women who looked like men and persons who looked like neither. It was early evening; he realized that most of the people were animals prowling on the hunt, seeking their night's prey. Later, he guessed, this international rodent population would go underground back into the bars and the private clubs, the stinking sewers that gave them their nourishment. A tender person stood in front of him wearing a low-cut dress and a vermilion skirt slashed to the waist. It carried a fox fur over its shoulder and its eyes and lips were heavily made up. 'Francais? American? English?' it said, in what it thought was a provocative voice.

'Piss off,' Regan said. He turned into the bar called The

Monte Carlo. The shrill voice followed him. 'Oh, that's what you like, is it?' A counter down the left of the room. On the right, seats shaped like half moons each with a table in front of it. A number of men were sitting at the bar. Regan found a stool with two empty ones on each side and hoisted himself on it. The waiter came along the bar, stood in front of Regan and yawned without saying anything, idly polishing a glass.

'When you wake up I'd like a beer,' Regan said. 'That's if you can spare the time.'

'Watch it,' the barman said, 'or they could be scraping you off a wall.' He turned and looked down the bar. The man sitting at the end of it round the bend had the face of an unsuccessful boxer. 'We've got an English comedian here, Hans,' he said. Hans grunted and muttered something Regan couldn't understand, but the gesture with which he finished his glass tankard of beer and set it on the bar close to his hand was unmistakable. Regan had been so busy watching the two of them, he hadn't seen the other one approach.

A hand that felt like a lead pipe rested on his shoulder. 'Nichts jokes,' a voice growled in his ear, 'this is a serious family place. You come, you drink. You stop drink, you go.' Regan turned. The man behind him could have been the brother of the one sitting further along the bar, eighteen stones of solid bone and muscle and doubtless a brain to match.

'Okay, okay, okay,' Regan said, wondering if his two shoulders could ever be the same height again.

He sat and drank, sipping the beer to pace himself. It tasted stronger and maltier than British beer. Every time he emptied a glass and set it down another one appeared in front of him. Though the barman was still yawning he never let a single empty glass except the pot of the bouncer remain on the bar for five seconds. Persons came, took a drink, and went. The seats either side of him filled and emptied again with the constant restless stream of persons looking for a soulmate. Regan kept his eyes strictly ahead observing the bar through the mirror which ran along its length, never turning his head. It hadn't taken him long to realize that he was the only 'straight' male in the whole place. After about half an hour an incredibly beautiful girl – a live, truly female, feminine doll – came and sat beside him. She had been sitting in one of the alcoves with another female, who was dressed in a navy blue pin-striped suit with a shirt and a tie, her hair in a crew cut. Regan had heard the booming laugh of the crewcut change to a sort of whining but loudmouthed petulance, though of course he couldn't understand the dialogue. When the pretty girl-type girl came to sit beside him, crewcut followed and the argument grew heavy. At its height the girl turned to him, touched his arm and said something Regan couldn't understand.

'I'm only here for the beer,' he said. 'Too bad it's not Double Diamond.'

The girl laughed. 'Ah, English,' she said. 'You buy me a drink?' Before he had a chance to refuse, a cocktail had been placed on the bar in front of the girl.

'Now you get the idea,' the barman said. 'Be happy, make friends. Not jokes!'

Crewcut slapped her hand petulantly on the bar and looked murderously at Regan. 'Du . . . du . . . *Mann*!', she said. It was the worst insult she could think of as she turned on her heel and marched out of the bar.

The girl with Regan went into a paroxysm of laughter and had to hold a handkerchief to her lips to stifle her near hysteria. 'My friend not like you,' she said. 'But I like you. I think you strong. Proper man. Not like others here.'

'I'm flattered, darling,' Regan said. 'You're a good looking piece yourself. But what a waste, what a waste . . .'

'A *waste*? How you mean?'

'Look, I'm straight, me. I'm dead normal. I don't go for this AC/DC lark. That's why it's a waste. You're a smashing looking piece, and any other way I'd have you out of that door and into bed faster than you can say einsweidry. But not if that's the kind of friends you have, the sort of company you keep.'

The handkerchief was in front of her mouth again, a delicate female touch, a dab at her lips, but this time, when she spoke, her voice was a whisper. 'Hello, Inspector Regan,' she said. 'I'm

Inspector Mainz. Funny, I heard all British coppers were poufs!'

'You cheeky bugger . . .'

'Order another drink,' she whispered, 'and then suggest in a louder voice that we go sit in one of the booths.'

Her English was as perfect as her figure and complexion.

Inspector Mainz saw Regan looking at her as they crossed the room and sat in the booth furthest from the door of the bar.

'They tell me your name is Jack,' she said.

'Yes.'

'Mine is Ingrid . . .'

'I thought that name came from further north.'

'Ah, big-breasted blonde-haired beauties from Sweden.'

'You don't do so bad yourself but, like I said, it's a waste.'

They were sitting close enough together to justify the pick-up in the eyes of anyone who might be watching, but Ingrid knew Jack Regan had put a barrier between them.

'I work under cover,' she said. 'Specializing in this district. My friend Olga, the one with the crewcut, she's undercover, too.'

'You didn't tell me! Bloody good actress. She could have fooled me. You too.'

'With Olga, that part comes easy. She doesn't like men. She likes young good-looking girls. But don't make any mistakes – she's a good policewoman, one of the toughest and the best.'

'And you? I guess it comes easy with you, too?'

She dropped her hand and held it tight on the bulge in his trousers, smiling at the shocked expression on his face. 'If you believe that, you'll believe anything,' she said. 'Like you, I'm normal. The AC/DC bit, as you call it, is something I put on for the villains.' She bit her fingernails into him and he grimaced with pain. 'I don't often switch off,' she said, 'but when I do, if I do, watch out.'

'And that's another bloody waste,' he said.

'What is . . .?'

'I think you've just ruined me for life.'

'I'm looking for a pipeline,' Regan said. 'I think one end of it starts here in Hamburg, and the other end finishes in London.'

'Harwich?'

'Up country from there.'

'Then why shouldn't this end of the pipeline start down country from the city of Hamburg itself.'

'Maibock,' Regan said, watching her face.

'Maibock. What about it? If you want a drink, he doesn't sell it here. There are just a few kneipes and liquor stores where you can find it. Anyway, I think it's all finished; it's only sold in May, you know. They put up posters with a ram's head on them. Now the posters are down.'

'But it is only sold in Hamburg?'

'Yes, so far as I know.'

'One of the corpses, no, two of them, had the remains of this maibock stuff in their stomachs.'

'Then they must have been in Hamburg. In the city.'

'It wouldn't make sense to bring them in here, then take them out again to feed them into the pipeline. Do you know the Tiger?'

'Yes. Funny you should mention that. I had a snout he was here in Hamburg. We made a set-up but we missed him.'

'He was in England. Then he came back to do that bank in Bremen.'

'If I could get him . . .!'

'*If* you could get him . . .?'

'I'd make Chefinspektor.'

'I think he comes down the pipeline.'

'I could ask around. How do you feel like a – what do you call it? – a pub crawl?'

'With you?'

'I don't suggest with Olga . . .'

'I'm getting to like this Koenigsberger Pils,' Regan said. 'With this head on it, it looks like stout.'

'Watch it; it can be lethal.'

'How many have I had?'

'If you don't remember, you've already had more than your ration. You'd better go on to Sangrita.'

'What the hell's that?'

'Tomato juice with chili peppers.'

'Yuk!'

In each of the countless bars and clubs they'd visited, the pattern had been the same. Ingrid had been greeted in each one by ribald comments when they had seen her companion; though Regan had not been able to understand the words, the implications had been clear. 'Who's this "straight" guy you're with for a change?' Ingrid's retorts had been good humoured but, apparently, pungent. It was obvious she was well known throughout the quarter, and that no-one suspected the true nature of her position. In every bar or club, Ingrid had looked carefully about at the clientele then had left Regan to go to talk to someone, a close tête-à-tête that in each case produced a quick shake of the head, usually a worried look, often the instant departure of the person concerned. It took the third Sangrita to get the result Ingrid had hoped for. They were in a a club called – The Pussy. The man Ingrid chose to talk to was obviously homosexual, but not as blatant as many of the others. He was sitting alone in a booth, watching everything that was going on without seeming to do so. It was a look Regan had been trained to spot, an alertness, a detailed knowledge of the surroundings and the people. Ingrid asked her questions, the man rubbed his thumb and forefinger together in an international gesture. Unlike all the others, he didn't look scared, didn't shake his head, didn't get up to go. Regan watched him in the mirror knowing that, though the man hadn't actually looked at him, he knew every detail of Regan's appearance. Ingrid asked the man a question; the man didn't reply but looked pointedly in Regan's direction. Though Regan could hear none of the dialogue, and it would have meant nothing to him anyway in German, he could almost write a script. Few 'snouts' will talk in the presence of a third party. He came off the stool, put a lurch into his steps, not a hard thing to do with all that pils inside him, and went across to the booth where they were sitting.

'I thought you and me was supposed to be together,' he said, deliberately slurring his voice. 'If you're not sitting and drinking with me, I might as well piss off . . .'

She looked at him, cold as ice. 'Why don't you do that,' she said. 'There are just as many fish in the sea.'

He turned and walked away, with the step of a man who knows he's had too many but is determined not to show it. When he got to the bar he took out a bundle of deutschmarks and fumbled them on to the counter. The bar man took one, shook his head, and placed the change beside the other notes.

'You have luck,' he said, 'that I no robber be. Put the money in the pocket. Go at once to the house.'

'I go,' Regan said, 'at once to the house. I do not pass "Go", I do not collect two hundred pounds.'

The people standing at the bar made room for him as he walked majestically past them. On the pavement outside, he turned right and walked slowly along, shedding his assumed drunkenness step by step.

Carter fell in beside him and whispered. 'You're being tailed, guv'nor. Man in a blue pin-stripe with a crew-cut.'

Regan chuckled. 'You've led a sheltered life, Carter,' he said. 'That's not a man. It's a woman!'

'Bloody hell . . . I could have sworn . . .'

'Like I said, you've led too sheltered a life.'

Regan walked slowly round the block until he came back to the corner from which he could see the club he'd just left. Two doors down was a window, open to the street. Above it was a sign that read, 'Wuerstchen'. Regan walked along to the window and his nostrils were assailed by the smells of sausages, frying chips, and another odour he couldn't recognize until he saw the tray of curry. 'You don't happen to have any fish-and-chips?' he asked the man serving behind the counter.

'Fish'n'chips? Nein Bratwurst, Wienerwurst, Kalbsbratwurst, Pommes Frites . . . ?'

'Sausage and chips. That one.'

The man took the bratwurst Regan had indicated, laid it in a paper tray, split it down its length and, before Regan could stop him, slopped the curry sauce into the gash. He gave Regan a separate tray of chips, and Regan paid, then leaned against the side of the building, eating.

He'd been there ten minutes when Ingrid left the club. Olga stayed where she was, on the other corner. Carter was fifty yards down the cross street behind Olga. Ingrid paused a moment on the doorstep outside the club, then turned and walked towards the corner where Olga was waiting. She went past without acknowledging Olga, and Regan started to walk along the pavement parallel with her. After two intersections, Ingrid turned and crossed the road to Regan's side.

'You've managed to sober up, then?' she said smiling. 'That was a good idea of yours, pretending to be drunk and walking out on me like that. He'd never have said a word so long as you were there.'

'That's what I thought.'

They turned the corner, walked up a few yards and she stopped at a doorway, the key already in her hand. They went in, climbed the stairs in front of them, and turned into the first floor flat. Regan looked about him while she took off her coat.

'Make yourself at home,' she said.

The room was about ten yards by seven, filled with the oddest collection of furniture he'd ever seen. Much of it was positively old, though not what you'd call antique. Some of it belonged to the tasteless post-war period, plastic and tubular steel. Some of it appeared to have been handmade, like the sofa, for example, which occupied both sides of one corner, and had a back of crudely painted tongue and groove boarding. On the right of the room was a large opening, at least four yards wide, with a woollen curtain suspended from an old-fashioned brass rod with rings and decorated end-pieces. The curtain was open wide, revealing a double mattress on the floor.

'I haven't yet found a bed I like,' Ingrid said as she came from the bedroom and saw the direction of his eyes. 'A mattress on the floor does for me. I'll make us some coffee.'

Regan sat in a large velvet covered armchair beneath a lamp of heavy bronze with a three feet crimson shade on it. 'That was an operating room lamp,' Ingrid said. 'I found it outside the hospital.'

'Found it?'

'Ah, you don't know our Hamburg habit. All this furniture is found. In Hamburg, anything you don't want, you put outside on the pavement on a certain day of each month. Then people wander around with prams and push-carts and wheelbarrows and help themselves. Anything left the next morning is taken away by the City Cleansing Department, and burned. That's how I got all this furniture. All free. But I'm waiting – one of these days, I'm going to find a four poster bed, with posts and curtains. I've always fancied myself in a four poster.'

Regan took his coffee and said nothing, though his thoughts were heavy and he felt a tightening in his gut. She sat in a wooden straight-backed rocking chair.

'Business first,' she said. 'There *is* a pipeline. A very expensive and exclusive way to travel. Gorgeous George . . .'

'Who?'

'Gorgeous George. The last man I was talking to. After you'd gone he opened up. One way ticket to England. No passport required. Five to ten thousand deutschmarks.'

'That's a lot of money . . .'

'But they get it.'

'How does it work?'

She shook her head. 'He wouldn't tell me that. But he did give me the name of the contact.'

'Who, I suppose, is a cut out? Don't call us, we'll call you . . .'

'That's right.'

'Do you know the contact?'

'Sure. He's a well-known villain. Petty crime. I'd say he

spent half his life inside before he got wise. Now he's just a contact man for all sorts of villainy. You want to unload a lorry of cut price cigarettes – he's the man you see. You want a half a dozen girls for an all night party in the Vier Jahreszeiten or any other of the big hotels – you know, private suite – he's the man to arrange the girls. He's what you'd call – a Fixer. Nowadays his nick-name is Freddie Ten Percent. The only thing he doesn't touch is any kind of drugs.'

'Thank God for small mercies. Where do we find him? Here on the Reeperbahn?'

'No, he's grown too grand for that. He has part shares in a Kneipe on Steindamm, near the railway station.'

'Near where I live.'

'That's right.'

Regan had been looking at her while she was talking. It was a look both of them recognized, that said – 'I'm a big boy now!'

'Do you want another drink?' she asked.

'No.'

'Coffee?'

'No, thanks.'

She got up, stretched. He watched her. 'It's been a long day,' she said. He nodded, came out of the chair and put his arms round her. She bent back her head and gazed far into his eyes. He kissed her lightly, on the mouth.

'I don't go for the "this thing is bigger than both of us" bit,' he said.

'Neither do I . . .'

'Good.' He took away his arms, walked into the bedroom through the alcove, efficiently stripped to his underpants, and lay on top of the eiderdown. She went round the room turning out the lights one by one.

'It's like that old Cary Grant and Myrna Loy film, run backwards,' he said. '*She* went round turning the lights *on* . . .'

She came into the bedroom out of the darkened sitting room, all her clothing left behind her.

'God, you're beautiful,' he said.

He didn't speak for another hour. Neither did she.

The grey light of a drizzling dawn filtered through the windows. He woke from a short but satisfying sleep to find her perched on one elbow looking down at him.

'How many people know you're here?' she asked, 'not here in this flat. Here in Hamburg?'

'Only your people at the Davidswache, and my people in London. Why?'

'You were followed when you came out of your pension to meet me this evening. Lucky I'd put Olga on to you, when they told me from the Davidswache to make a quiet contact with you.'

'Oh, him! That's my sergeant. Good God, I forgot to tell him to go home. He'll still be . . .'

Ingrid had burst out laughing. 'Come and look,' she said. She crawled across the floor below the level of the windowsill and together they looked out beneath the open curtain. Carter was standing in a doorway on one corner, and Olga was standing in a doorway on the other. 'I told Olga to tail him,' Ingrid said. 'Not to let him out of her sight. I thought he was a villain.'

She couldn't get to sleep. Lit a cigarette, the first one he'd ever seen her smoke; made a cup of coffee. 'That'll keep you awake even longer,' he said, resting his elbow, looking at her. What a sod police work could be. Ingrid was young and alive, uncannily beautiful and with a good brain. She ought to be out in the daylight, married to some high-ranking guy, having kids, maybe even working in a job as a highly paid executive. Instead of which, she spent her days in bed, her nights skulking around gay and lesbian bars, ingratiating her way into that half world which acted as a nest for so many criminal activities.

'What did you do this evening before you got in contact with me?' he asked.

'We got a drug pusher we've been after for months. Olga

caught a man who's been on her personal wanted list all year – a guy who's been raping young girls. We found out where Joe the Finger is hiding out after that bank job on the Wiesingerweg. Now we have it under surveillance, and we'll get the whole gang, one by one. We've even got a line on the loot, two million deutschmarks. And, last but not least, we've cracked the blackmailer's case. Or I think we have.'

'The blackmailer's case?'

'Yes. Business men from abroad. Wandering down the Reeperbahn looking for what they call fun and games. Wind up with a girl in a back room. Girl turns out to be a boy, lots of photographs taken with infra-red. The business man pays up, every time.'

'More fools them for pissing about in the Reeperbahn. I have no patience with that kind of stupid bugger . . .'

'Its my *patch* – is that what you call it? My territory. I can't let it happen here. The Reeperbahn already has a bad enough name.'

'You've had a busy night?'

'About average.'

'And you're not tired . . .?'

'Not *too* tired!'

The latest edition of the *Hamburger Abendblatt* carried a bold story on its front page. 'Well-known Australian criminal arrested. Held for extradition to Australia. Wanted for robbery with violence.'

The *Bild-Zeitung*, the German equivalent of the *Daily Mirror*, carried a similar story the following morning, though now the *criminal* was known as a gangster and extortionist, a racketeer and an underworld gangleader, said to control the Sydney waterfront Mafia.

The photograph used in both stories was the same. A mug shot of Jack Regan.

Regan was still awake when Ingrid came home around two o'clock in the morning. 'The fish are nibbling at the bait,' she said. 'Gorgeous George came up to me tonight. Told me I kept dangerous company. He recognized you from the newspaper reports.'

'Good. What did you tell him?'

'That you were too tough to be inside for long. That you'd either escape or buy some high-powered legal help. Or twist somebody's arm.'

'Good. So he knows I'm not short of bread?'

'Bread . . .?'

'You speak such good English I forget, sometimes. Bread, dough, moulah, bees-and-honey, money.'

'You English. Sometimes I despair.'

She snuggled into bed beside him. 'I hope this case of yours lasts for a very long time,' she said. 'It's good to have a real man to come home to. Olga has her uses, but sometimes . . . This curious half world I live in gets to me. I begin to wonder if I'm going queer, too.'

'No worry about that,' he said. 'Like me, you're normal.'

There was an added urgency and fierceness in their love making as if she was trying to reassure herself. 'Take it easy,' he said, 'you don't need to prove anything, either to me or yourself.'

Modest headlines in the *Hamburger Abendblatt* chauvinistically announced – 'Foreign criminal escapes from Australian police escort on way to the airport'.

The *Bild-Zeitung* followed with a banner headline – 'Mad-dog killer at large again'.

Die Morgenpost reprinted the picture next to that of a young lady, unclothed, who appeared to be having difficulty covering her large breasts with the wisps of her long blond hair. Unfortunately, the captions had been crossed and Regan appeared as 'Local beauty has trouble with the wind', while the girl, it warned, 'May have a concealed weapon'.

Another sleepless night. 'Why do you do it?' Regan asked. 'With your record, you could choose any job on the force.'

Ingrid couldn't answer. Now that they'd shared a greater intimacy he could detect the fine lines behind the smooth and still lovely, features, could see the feeling deep in her eyes. He stroked the side of her nose.

'It's often been said, but this time, it's true. You're not just a pretty face. So why do you do it? And do you consider what it's doing to you? When you make love, you're a tigress . . .'

'You don't seem to object . . .'

'I don't. As the Yankees would say, you're a fantastic lay. A right screamer. Afterwards, I don't fall asleep. I pass out, exhausted. Like I've been put through a wringer. You're every man's dream, both in bed and out. So why the Reeperbahn, at night, with a bunch of queers and lesbians, pimps, prostitutes, all the human shit . . .?'

'That's the point,' she said. She sat up in bed and hugged her knees, her taut flesh gleaming in the soft glow of the lamp she always insisted on having alight while they made love. 'They're not *all* human shit. Some of them are, some I wouldn't turn over with a spade and spread on a "Schrebergarten". They're evil, perverted, twisted, sick. I'd put them all, men and women, into a special prison and throw away the key. Look, I had a brother once. At thirteen he was as good looking as you seem to think I am. He was picked up by an old cruiser who taught him the queer tricks. Dammit, at thirteen, he didn't know any different. Then the cruiser put him on drugs. My brother walked off a roof before his fourteenth birthday, blown out of his mind on heroin.'

'I'm bloody sorry, Ingrid,' Regan said. 'I didn't mean to open old sores.'

'You're not. I've been over it for a long time. My first underground job was getting the cruiser.'

'He was arrested . . .?'

'Don't you believe it,' she said, and now he could see her mouth set in a hard line. 'When I'd nailed him, I spread the word around that he was an informer. We didn't need to arrest him. They had to stick him together again to bury him. He was one of what you call, the shit. There've been lots more like him, male and female, and I've chased them with a passion. And been very lucky. That's why I made Inspektor, even though I've a low record of actual arrests. When I get a big one, somehow, they just seem to disappear out of circulation. Permanently. That way I don't have to give evidence in court, and my cover is never blown.'

'A one-woman clean-up campaign?'

'Call it that.'

'And the rest? The non-shitty ones?'

'That's my problem. Look, there's no point in me being modest. I know, I've always known, that when the femininity bit was being dished out, I got more than my share. All my life, I've been fighting men off. And it's been a load of fun. I've enjoyed myself. I've always been able to have the fellows everybody else wanted, the tall dark handsome guys with the good teeth and the wavy hair. I could have had a big house in Blankenese, servants, a big yacht. I was even propositioned by a real-life Prince from Munich.'

'And, instead, you wind up in bed with me . . .?'

'Don't sell yourself short, Regan. You're alive. Money kills, you know, it's a poison people hold in their hands. It seems to make them anaemic, and that's the last thing anybody could say about you.'

'I wouldn't want to try giving a transfusion right now.'

'If it was needed, you'd provide it. You're like me, Regan. You've got what you need, when you need it. It's precisely because I've got what I need, and more, that I feel so bloody sorry for the people who don't have it. And that's ninety-five per cent of the people on the Reeperbahn. The people who lack femininity, and become lesbians in self-defence.'

'Like Olga.'

'Right first time. People who lack self-confidence. Men who've always been too shy to make it with a woman, and find it a lot easier to let another man make it with them. There are two sorts on the Reeperbahn, the deprived, and the depraved. And they're not both the same, though one feeds off the other.'

'And you've got a one-woman campaign going to help the deprived and stamp out the depraved is that it?'

'Not a one-woman campaign, as you call it. There are one or two of us. We have a marvellous Chief, a woman, who thinks like we do.'

Talking to him seemed to have helped her. He pulled her gently down into the bed, put his arm around her. Soon, she fell asleep while he stared into the dawn.

Superintendent Maynon blew his stack. 'Ten thousand deutschmarks?' he said. 'Where do you think we're going to get money like that, transferred to you in Hamburg. What the hell are you and Carter doing there, that needs ten thousand deutschmarks. Don't you know the pound has taken a nose-dive down to one dollar fifty-two?'

'So make up your mind, Superintendent. Do you want that pipeline blocked, or don't you? The German police are prepared to co-operate this end, but they can't be expected to pay my fare back to England, can they?'

'I'll pay your fare back. £25 on the *Prinz Hamlet*. And for that, you can even get an inside cabin . . .'

'So Chief Haskins has been doing your homework for you, Super.'

'We need some check on your paperwork, dammit.'

The Super went on grumbling for a further ten minutes before, finally, he agreed.

Ingrid collected the money from the Dresdner Bank, off the Reeperbahn. The paying out clerk told her that, if she cared to wait a short while until they closed, he'd walk her home to protect her.

'It's a large sum of money,' he said. 'I wouldn't like you to get robbed. On the way, we could have a cup of coffee . . .' Ingrid eyed his sweaty hands.

'If the choice is being robbed or pawed,' she said sweetly, 'I think I'd rather be robbed.'

Freddie Ten Percent looked like Franz Josef Strauss, with jelly roll double chins, a heaving belly, and hands like stuffed entrails. His small pig-like eyes were set close together on the bridge of his large, florid nose, the end of which he continually wiped on the sleeve of his jacket. 'Whatever makes you think, dearie, that I know anything about that sort of thing?' he asked plaintively. 'Honest, people come to me for everything. People are always bothering me for simply everything.'

He smiled at her. 'Now, if you wanted to go into business for yourself,' he said. 'That's something I *do* know something about. I have lots of friends. Very nice, steady, important business men. From all over Europe. A lot of them come here to do really big business deals. They could use a social secretary. Someone of your grace and charm would fit in very well. You could earn a couple of hundred deutschmarks for just an evening's work . . .'

'Tarts on the Reeperbahn get that,' she said, matching his light tone.

'*Tarts?* Who said anything about *tarts*?'

Ingrid put a one thousand deutschmark note on the table in front of her. Freddie's eyes flicked down and up again, then opened as wide as was possible. 'Rich little bitch, aren't we?' he said. She could see his hands squirming, no doubt itching to touch the money.

She picked up the note. 'My friend wants to take a journey,' she said. 'He has five thousand deutschmarks. He would like to see the Changing of the Guard at Buckingham Palace, only he's misplaced his passport. Five thousand deutschmarks, just to see the Changing of the Guard. In cash. And the notes are watermarked. But, if you don't want to help him . . .?' She was going to put the note back into her pocket but, despite its flabby bulk, his hand shot out like the head of a cobra and touched hers, cold and clammy.

'I didn't say I didn't *want* to help,' he said. 'But it might be, shall we say, difficult. I hear you have some very interesting friends. Some very, shall we say, well-known friends. He might have to travel first class, if he's the man I think he is, and you know what that means.'

'How much?'

'I don't know until you tell me who he is.'

'Hans Schmidt . . .'

'Ha, you will have your little joke. Strange how many men ask to do business with me called Hans Schmidt.'

'Without a passport, who can tell?'

He reached inside the folds of his jacket and produced a fat wallet. From it he extracted a folded newspaper cutting with the caption, 'Mad-dog killer at large again'. 'Let me give you an instance,' he said. 'A man like this would have to travel luxury class. I doubt it could be done much under ten thousand.'

'Top price.'

'If, dearie, if . . .'

'But you'll see what you can arrange?'

He held up his hands in horror. '*Arrange*, me? I arrange nothing. I'm merely speculating. I know nothing about anything, absolutely nothing. I imagine what would happen, in such a case, would be that the person concerned would have to give a telephone number, or an address, and he'd be contacted there. You understand, I don't *know*. I'm just, how can I put it, surmising.'

'And your surmise would cost me . . .'

'Who said anything about costing you anything. We're just having a little friendly discussion. If you'd care to buy me a drink, I'm too much of a gentleman to say no. I think that should just about cover it.' His hand fastened on the thousand deutschmark note, which disappeared into its folds of fat. Ingrid gently reached out her hand and stroked the back of his.

'Just so we understand each other,' she said. Where her hand had caressed his, a thin line of blood welled up, a cross carved delicately into his skin. 'I didn't reach this age without knowing how to take care of myself,' she said. 'And my enemies, too!'

The technician from the Fernsprechamt finished the installation of the extra telephone in Ingrid's apartment ten minutes after Ingrid returned home. 'Anything to sign?' Ingrid asked.

The man looked puzzled. 'They told me there was no paperwork,' he said. 'So far as anyone knows, this phone doesn't exist. Queer! I've never put one in like this before. You could call China on that phone and it wouldn't cost you. I asked the supervisor, but he didn't know anything about it, either. Just said it was a special.'

When Ingrid had got rid of him, Regan came out of the bedroom where he had been hiding. He was nervous and irritable. 'Poor Regan,' she said. 'You don't enjoy being cooped up in here all day, do you?'

He grunted. 'It's all in a good cause,' he said, 'The last thing I want is to be seen on the street and turned in by an irate citizen as the Mad-dog killer.'

Both stood stock still. The new telephone was ringing. 'You answer that one,' Ingrid whispered.

Regan picked it up and with no attempt to disguise his voice, read the number on the dial in English. He listened for a while then put the phone down. 'That's odd,' he said. 'I read the number and a voice on the other end said, "Excuse me. This is the Post Office. We've received a report of a fault on your line, but it seems to be all right now. Sorry to have troubled you!" They spoke in English . . .'

Ingrid's face shone. 'It's working,' she said, 'It's working . . .'

The new telephone rang again, at four o'clock in the morning. A hard metallic voice said. 'Do you have nine thousand deutschmarks?'

'Yes, I have them.'

'Good. Be ready to move at any time. No luggage, understand. And that means no guns, knives, nothing. Don't use this phone, ever. If we try to ring this number and the line is engaged, the deal is off and you lose your deposit, right?'

'I understand.'

'Next time we ring, it'll be a short call. Just an address. Get there as fast as you can, but in any case, not later than one hour after we call or else . . .'

'The deal is off and I lose my deposit.'

'Say, Englishman . . .'

'Australian . . .'

'Have it your way. You're catching on, quick.'

'That's why I'm still alive and a lot of other people aren't.'

'Okay, tough guy. Don't use the phone and wait for the call.'

'When?'

'Who knows?'

'I'm a patient man, up to a point. But I have a thousand invested. A man could lose his balls, if that investment went sour on me.'

'Good. Now hang up the phone. And don't pick it up again until it rings.'

Regan did as he was told. Ingrid was still on the other telephone, listening hard. After a few moments she put it down. 'Damn,' she said. 'Damn and blast! That bastard talked long enough to get his message through and to verify the phone wasn't tapped, but just not long enough for us to trace the call.'

'Forget it,' Regan said. 'They're professionals.'

Now that Regan was under starter's orders, and Ingrid knew it, a terrible desperation came into her love-making as if, for the first time, she'd met a soul that blended with her own and was desperate to draw whatever strength she could from it, before it was too late. And Regan was aware that, in some deep psychological way, he was being used. Regan was neither a deep nor psychological man but he could clearly sense this mood of desperation. They were sitting in bed after a particularly demanding bout; Regan had made coffee and had bought it back to the bed where Ingrid, sated for the moment and exhausted, was lying flat on her face white and drawn but not, he knew, entirely with physical exertion. Though there'd been plenty of that the last few hours. He offered her one of her cigarettes, which she refused with a tired shake of her head.

'Look Ingrid,' he said, 'this is no business of mine and normally I'm like a mouse with a trap when it comes to sticking my nose in. But this job of yours, here on the Reeperbahn. It's killing you. You're too involved to do a job like that. Why the hell don't you get yourself shifted. Get on the Robbery Squad, some straightforward job like that . . .'

'Then find a nice guy and settle down, get married, have a house in Volksdorf, a bunch of kids . . .?'

'No need to go to extremes . . .'

'Would *you* marry me, Regan? Would you settle down with me? They're recruiting a new International Squad here. Man with your experience could start near the top. I could teach you German.'

'Yes, well, I was married, once.'

'I guessed you had been. What did she do, start checking your change every night, turning out your pockets? Or did she want you to take her out once in a while, go and have tea with her Mother on a Sunday? She should have known better from a Schupo . . .'

'The Reeperbahn is killing you.'

'It's killing everybody who hangs out there. One more won't be noticed. It's killing Olga. How do you think she feels, putting her hands on a villain who happens to be a pretty young blonde, wheeling her inside on a charge of pick-pocketing, drug possession, whatever and *fancying* her all the time she's making the arrest?'

'That's Olga's problem, not yours!'

'That's where you're wrong, Regan. Bloody wrong. It is *my* problem. It's everybody's problem. Sure, when we track down this pipeline, we'll pick up a few villains. Naughty boys are taking money for breaking a *law*, for aiding people to move about without passports. But what's so fucking criminal about that? You tell me most of the men they move are Pakistanis with fathers, mothers, brothers, sisters, kids, already in England. *Illegal* immigrants. *Illegal?* Whose bloody law? Not my law. I don't give a damn who goes to live anywhere. All it takes is a politician's vote to create a Common Market, whatever crap that may be, and all of a sudden, you can come into Germany and I can go into England any time we want. But the scum that floats along the Reeperbahn, they are illegal because they are fucking *immoral*. They're ruining the lives of people. Not stealing money from banks – who cares about that? Not taking away motor cars without insurance policies – again, who the hell cares about that? But they're pushing drugs, buggering young boys and girls, perverting normal lives with their blue movies and disgusting sex displays. Would you like what we've just done to each other to be shown on a blue movie screen . . .? Would you?' Her voice had risen until she was almost shouting at him.

'I don't make the laws,' he said. 'Neither do you. Our jobs, as coppers, is to make sure other buggers keep the laws of the land, whatever they may be . . .'

'That's a cop-out, Regan, and you know it.'

Now he was shouting, too. 'It's no more a cop-out,' he said, 'than hanging about the Reeperbahn like some bloody angel of mercy. You ought not to be in the police force. You ought to be in the Salvation Army, thumping a drum, singing, Come and Save Us . . .'

He caught the first punch she threw at him, but missed the second that landed square on his mouth. He felt the sweet rush of blood down his chin, reached for her wild hands, grabbed them and turned her round. She arched her body back at him; her mouth landed on his shoulder and her teeth bit in, deep. 'You bitch,' he howled. She snapped her head back, a fighting tiger, and the hardness of her skull beneath all that lovely hair, smashed into the bridge of his nose, flooding his eyes with tears and momentarily blinding him. Her leg had slid forward under the sheets and she bent her knee and snapped her foot back, hard into the pit of his stomach, moved it forward to hack at him again, this time adjusting her knee so that the blow would go lower.

The phone rang. The new phone.

Her foot came back and there was an explosion of pain between his legs that left him gasping. 'The phone's ringing,' he managed to grunt between the waves of nausea.

'Fuck it! Who cares . . .?' she said and drew her foot forward again.

'I do!' He released one of her hands, quickly raised his, and chopped down below her ear. Her head slumped on to the pillow.

'Sorry, love,' he said, as he hobbled across the floor. He picked up the phone and said the number.

'What kept you?'

'I was saying goodbye.'

The voice at the other end chuckled. 'I heard you were a boyo,' it said, the accent tinged with Irish. 'Can you get yourself to the Fish Market in an hour. That'll be six o'clock, local time.'

'Whereabouts in the Fish Market?'

'Oh, just saunter along the quayside, as if you hadn't a care in the world and somebody will contact you. They'll be tapping you on the shoulder, I expect, so don't move too hasty, will you? I wouldn't like any of my lads to be getting a black eye, now would I? Just one other tiny detail, cobber, isn't that what you say down under? You'll not forget to bring the boodle with you, will you? And you'll make sure there's nobody sitting on your tail, won't you?'

'I wasn't born yesterday.'

'I guessed you weren't. Right, cobber, see you soon. One last thing. Don't get back into bed to say any more goodbyes. You might fall asleep and miss the boat. There's lots of pussy in London. Oddly enough, a lot of it watching the Changing of the Guard, outside Buckingham Palace. Right, put down the telephone, there's a good lad.'

The Saviem Arctic had travelled a few kilometres past the last Hanover turn-off; Arthur Naylor was driving when Sam Little, who'd been sleeping in the comfortable bunk in the back of the cabin, stretched and got out, climbing over the back of the passenger seat. He poured water from the container into a bowl he held between his knees, rinsed his face and then cleaned his teeth before dumping the water out of the window of the cab. Arthur Naylor had been watching all this time dividing his attention between Sam Little and the motorway which stretched, seemingly endlessly, ahead. The Innsbruck run had been an easy one with absolutely no difficulties at any border or at the unloading point. When Sam had finished his ablution Arthur obviously made up his mind to speak.

'Sam,' he said, 'I wonder if I could ask you a favour?'

'You want me to drive? Sure, I don't mind.'

'No, it's not that.' Arthur knew Sam was an easy-going type, but a bit of a snot nose who did everything by the book. Well, of course, it was right he should – they all knew Sam had two strikes against him and Pat Booth had taken a chance by employing him. Sam repaid Pat Booth by trying never to step out of line even in the smallest matter. 'I've been doing this Hamburg run for a long time,' Arthur said. 'Fact is, I've got to know a girl.'

'A girl? And you a married man with kids.' It was hard to tell if Sam was joking or not, if he approved or not. 'Yes, well, my missus and me we haven't had much in common since the last kid was born. To tell you the truth, I've got my own bedroom at home. Well then, I met this girl, see, and it all fits in very nicely.'

'You dirty devil.'

'No, you clot, I don't mean fits in like that. You see, she's got a job with one of the airlines and she doesn't want to get married or anything. Well, what I'm getting at is . . .'

'I'm not a bloody priest, you know Arthur, you don't have to make any confessions to me. All right, you found a bird in Hamburg and you want to spend the night with her. I can look after the truck on my own, you know. Anyway, there's nothing in it. We're coming back empty so there's no fear of our load being hijacked.'

'Well, it's not exactly that,' Arthur said. 'You remember I told you this girl works for an airline. So, you see, she can get free tickets. What I usually do – what I've been doing when I've been riding with Tooley – is to stay the two nights, you see – the night we get in to Hamburg and then the next night while you're on board the *Prinz Hamlet*. And then my bird fixes me a flight to Gatwick. You dock at nine, you see, and I get a flight that gets me into Gatwick at nine. Then I get the train to London and a tube out and you pick me up on your way round the North Circular. It means of course, that you have to look after the truck here in Hamburg, get it on board and off again on your own and take it up to the North Circular on your own. I used to give Mark Tooley a couple of quid.' He paused. 'I could make it three quid and you can have my duty frees as well . . .?'

Sam Little felt the relief flood through him and realized why Seamus O'Brien – however he managed to do it – had fixed Arthur Naylor as his co-driver. 'No, Arthur,' he said. 'You can keep your money. I'll be glad to help out. Call it the romantic streak. I always did like playing Cupid.'

'Thanks a lot,' Arthur said. 'Tell you what. When we get to the depot I'll do all the paperwork and you can leave all the washing down to me and get home to your missus!'

'Now there's an offer I can't very well refuse,' Sam said.

Regan came out of the building in which Ingrid had her apartment and turned sharp right walking quickly. After fifteen paces he did a fast about-turn and started to walk in the other direction. It's an old trick. It flushed out Olga, who'd been sitting in the front of a parked van. Thank God Carter, London-trained, had stayed where he was, at the driving wheel of the Volkswagen Minibus, parked on the cross street. Two professionals – one not quite so professional as the other. And one amateur. Now trapped into walking down the street towards Regan, on the same side. He turned and ducked into the doorway of a shop, but not before Regan had identified him. What had Ingrid called him – 'Gorgeous George'. Regan used one of the slanting windows of a shop to look behind him. Gorgeous George stepped out of the shop doorway not ten paces behind Regan. Rank bloody amateur he was!

Regan paused on the corner. The nearside blinker on the Volkswagen clicked three times. Regan didn't need to nod. Copper talk. 'Watch it, there's a man on your tail! On your side of the road.'

Once again Regan felt the sour taste on his tongue, the imminence of action. After days spent in that flat, he physically ached for it. Logical to suppose, wasn't it? He'd been seen with Ingrid, a known person. Somebody would have Ingrid's address. It would be worth putting a man outside the door, just in case. The mistake they'd made was to choose a bloody amateur. Olga had spotted George and was staying behind him. Carter was staying behind Olga. Regular bloody caravan.

Ingrid had still been out cold when he left her flat. Just as well. He hated goodbyes. Olga would make contact; somebody would be sent round to find out what had happened to Ingrid. She'd read the note he'd pinned to the pillow. 'Take my advice, and quit. And thanks for everything.'

He held up his hand for a cruising taxi which did a U-turn.

'That shop, Karstadt,' Regan said.

'Very good,' the driver said in heavily accented English. 'I've never counted them, but there must be, ungefaehr, thirty. Dreizig. Trente? Capisco?'

'You sound like the bloody United Nations. The one across the Reeperbahn!'

'Now you're talking, baby.'

They travelled two minutes in blissful silence then the driver adjusted his mirror. 'Hey, you English? I was in England during the war. Prisoner-of-war. Worked on a farm. Learned English pretty good, eh? Lots of lovely chicks. Yes, I really got screwed.'

'No more than you deserved, I'm sure,' Regan said. 'Is there a radio in this thing?'

'Sure have. You want the news? I can tell you what's happening.'

'Turn on the music!' Regan said, 'I feel like dancing.'

The cab stopped outside Karstadt. Regan paid the driver, got out, and stood on the pavement, looking down the Reeperbahn smiling at George's discomfiture. He'd got out of his cab, no doubt having paid in advance, and now was trying to get back in to avoid being seen by Regan. Unfortunately, two large matrons with shopping parcels were also trying to get in. Regan could hear the altercation from where he was standing. Bloody amateur! Olga in her van. Carter in the Volkswagen, sitting tight. Regan took out his handkerchief and blew his nose, knowing Carter would read that and stay where he was. He turned and hurried across the pavement and into the fan of hot air which took the place of a door. Turned right. Looked back out of the inside window. Olga! Olga! No wonder you never made Inspektor. She was out of the van and half-way across the street. Turn, walk quickly to the moving staircase. Run swiftly up it, turn round, across by the hardware department, down the stairs beside the bank of elevators. Across the ground floor. Out through the hot air curtain.

'Would you happen to have a light?' said a soft Irish voice he instantly recognized.

The driver of Olga's van clicked the shutter of her Nikon, recording the meeting between Regan and the Irishman. She ripped the film out of the camera, held her hand out of the window, and the spool was taken by a young fellow dressed in the uniform of a Rocker, the leather, studded jacket, the flying boots, the greasy leather trousers. The Rocker climbed on to a four cylinder BMW motor bicycle, pressed the kick start, and roared away through the traffic. Four minutes later, the film was in the police laboratories, in the high speed developer.

The negative, while still wet, was scanned by the computer reader and transferred on to a data base in the form of electrical impulses. It was then transmitted to Immigration Control, and to Interpol Headquarters in Paris. Immigration control pushed the signals through an electrostatic dry-copy line-linked printing machine which gave an enlargement on paper to every immigration control duty point. Among the other members of Interpol, the Special Branch at Scotland Yard in England, had a dry print, all within ten minutes of the picture being taken.

Sergeant Hargreaves was the Special Branch librarian on duty, one of a team of three men working round the clock, each with an encyclopaedic memory for names and faces. Hargreaves ripped the enlargement out of the machine, turned it over, and scribbled 'Seamus O'Brie(a)n?' on the back of it, before handing it to the Special Branch duty Officer.

'I've just had a multi-stations teleprint about that from Hamburg via Paris,' he said. 'Do we have a biography?'

Hargreaves smiled. 'I thought you'd be asking me,' he said and put a file on the Duty Officer's desk. 'I got it from the Irish Section.'

'With a name like O'Brien, you'd be hardly likely to look in the Israeli pool, now would you?'

'I don't smoke,' Regan said to the Irishman.

'That's very sensible. 'Tis awful bad for your health. Like rushing about crowded department stores.' They'd turned and were walking rapidly parallel with the store front. Where they turned the corner, a van was parked with its back open.

'Inside,' the Irishman said.

Regan walked straight in. The doors were slammed, and the van pulled away, Regan and Seamus facing each other, sitting on the wheel hubs.

'That should have got rid of them,' the Irishman said. 'Permit me to introduce myself. My name is Seamus O'Brien. I'm what you might call your friendly travel courier. And your name, if I'm not mistaken, is Thomas Chafferty, the scourge of New South Wales, the Mad-Dog Killer. Though, I must say, you don't sound very Australian to me . . .'

'Too bloody true, cobber. I was brought up in New Zealand.

South Island. British parents, who never went off the sheep farm! You get mortally sick of sheep, you know? Like those two bloody lambs who were following me.'

'Two?'

'Gorgeous George for one. I guess he also is a friendly travel courier.'

'I will say this for you, Mr Chafferty. You're a professional, every bit of it. You said the *two* little lambs . . .'

'Come off it. You were the second . . .'

'And so I was, dear boy, so I was. I just didn't want you to miss your way, and lose your deposit. You've brought the balance with you, I imagine? You being such a professional.'

Regan took a bundle of notes and handed them across. Seamus O'Brien's eyebrows lifted when he saw them. He held one up, or at least, half of one. The note had been torn neatly across the middle. He checked; all the notes had been torn and no halves matched.

'You get the other halves,' Regan said coolly, 'when I feel my feet on the good old soil of England . . .'

'You are a *romantic*, Mr Chafferty. Feet on the soil of England, indeed. Myself, I've always had a fascination for Rupert Brooke. "Some corner of a foreign field that is forever England." You wouldn't want to spend your immortal life buried in some corner of a foreign field, would you, Mr Chafferty? That's what'll happen if you play fun and games with a man like me.' The gun had come out of his overcoat pocket with the speed and ease of a cowboy's draw, Hollywood style. ' 'Tis a nasty little thing, this Mauser,' he said conversationally. 'Streamlined. Comes out of your pocket like a kid glove. But don't be deceived, will you; It's not exactly a toy. Trouble is, this seven-point-six-five ammunition is hard to come by and I don't like wasting it. I therefore never fire it unless I mean to kill somebody. And you wouldn't want that to happen, would you, just when you're starting a holiday trip to see the Changing of the Guard. I'll have the other half of the notes now.'

Regan slowly reached out his hand and, without deflecting Seamus's aim, put it round the barrel of the pistol. 'I'm a pro,' he said, 'and you're a pro. Put the gun away. I don't have the other halves of those notes on me. Do you think I'm a bloody fool? The money's safe as the Bank of Hamburg.'

'Good you didn't say the Bank of England.'

'But it's where neither you *nor* I can get it, until I reach England. And before you start waving that thing at me again, I don't know where it is. I shan't know, until we get to England.'

The Irishman thought for a moment or two, then slipped the gun back into his pocket. 'You're going to have to tell me more than that,' he said, 'before I let you travel.'

DDS Schedule D Confidential the teleprinter in Chef Inspektor Hassel's Office in the Davidswache printed on its platter.

DDS Schedule D Confidential the message was repeated. The operator sitting by the machine called out to the Chief Inspektor who came over. The Operator got up and stood back while the Chief sat down.

CI HASSEL 12/D/KKHAMBURG, Hassel slowly typed, then added *GA*.

The message came through, at the speed of the automatic tape, faster than any human fingers could have managed.

YOUR REQUEST 12DKKH2100 SEAMUS O'BRIEN NAT IRISH FATHER IRISH GERMAN MOTHER ANGLO IRISH AGE FORTY TWO POB CORK IRELAND NATIONALITY PASSPORT NO 1217456 ISSUED CORK 2 SEP 74 RENEW BUSINESS INTERESTS GRAVEL PITS AND PREMIX CONCRETE BLETCHLEY ENGLAND CATERING HAMBURG GERMANY FREQUENT TRAVELLER ENGLAND GERMANY IRELAND SUSPECTED IRA SYMPATHIZER SUSPECTED MAJOR FUND RAISER IRA SPECIAL BRANCH SURVEILLANCE CATEGORY D NOTE MOVEMENTS FOR FILE BUT DO NOT INTERCEPT NO RECORD ARRESTS DITTO CONVICTIONS MORE ON REQUEST OVER.

Hassel ripped the paper from the machine. 'Get a copy of that to Ingrid,' she said. 'You'll probably find her down the street in Wardrobe.'

She went to her desk, picked up the telephone, and dialled a number. 'A man called O'Brien, Seamus O'Brien, has a number of business interests here in Hamburg. We have a dossier on him from Special Branch in London. I want someone to locate all those business interests, and report the activities in each one. Just a report, you understand, nothing overt. And I wanted it on my desk five minutes ago.'

'There's not much to tell,' Regan said. 'When we arrive in England – and I guess we'll be travelling on the Hamburg–Harwich ferry?–'

Seamus made no comment.

'I'll get out of the truck on the main road out of Harwich. My lad will be watching. Through binoculars. If I look all right to him, he'll put the money into a sand-box further along beside the road. He'll park his car near the sand-box, but he won't be in it. If anyone else but me tries to take that money out of the sand-box, he'll fire the rifle he'll be looking down. Whoever is in the lorry will take the half notes from me, get back into the lorry, and sit there. I'll get into my lad's car and go. The man in the lorry will be free to drive away after five minutes.'

Seamus O'Brien was shaking his head with admiration. 'I've said it before, Mr Chafferty, but I'll say it again. You're a *professional*. 'Tis a pleasure to work with you. A sand-box on the side of the road. Whoever would have thought of that? There must be a hundred sandboxes on the side of the road, and nobody ever thinking of looking into one of them. It occurs to me, you could hide a dead body in a sand-box, and it would never be found until the next cold snap, the next frost on the road. You get my point, Mr Chafferty. It's either you, or the money, one of the two, in the sand-box. Let's hope for your sake, it's the money, the other halves of these nine thousand lovely deutschmarks.'

Regan grinned at him.

'There's just one little thing bothering me,' Seamus said, 'you being such a professional. You know, there were three people, following. Not two. Now, how do you account for that? You being a pro' an' all.'

Regan still grinned. 'Could it have been the friend of a friend, do you think? Wanting to wish me a bon voyage. Hoping that when I'd gone she could take over again where she left off?'

Seamus slapped his knee. 'You're right,' he said, 'Hell hath no fury . . .'

'Like an unplugged dyke?'

Seamus almost collapsed with laughter. 'An unplugged dyke? Man, you're not only a poet, you're a humorist, too.' When he sat up, however, his laughter had ended and the gun was back in his hand. 'We've arrived, cobber,' he said. 'Now do as I say and turn out your pockets, one by one, nice and slow.'

During the day a man can hardly move on the Fish Market alongside the Elbe where the fish cutters from the North Sea deliver their cargoes in boxes and baskets. The varied catch is sorted, graded, and weighed, stacked in heaps around which the sellers and buyers stand nodding their bids. The purchases are carted either into waiting vans and lorries or to the many retail stalls dotted about, where the grim nods of the professionals give way to stentorian shouts as stall holders compete for customers. It's a daytime scene of pandemonium, a tourist attraction, lorries, vans, and trucks constantly moving backwards and forwards under the eyes of cameras, the slime and slither of wet fish, the rap tap and clatter of clogs, the unphotographable but unforgettable stench without which no fish market could ever survive.

At the end of long days that begin at dawn, hosepipes are uncoiled, pavings are doused clean, cutters and carts, vans and lorries, buyers and sellers, stalls and their holders, all drift away into the Hamburg night. Then the gulls come looking for scraps, cats looking for both, tramps seeking a doss, drinkers a corner in which to piss, vomit, count what small change is left after the rapacious Reeperbahn, and wonder where the rest has gone, all gone.

Sam Little drove the Saviem along the side of the Elbe, passed the end of the loading ramp to the Prinz Hamlet ferry on which he would be driving in the morning. He turned the Saviem, as he had been instructed, on to the Fish Market, now dark and deserted. He got out of the cab and made sure the doors were locked. He went to the back of the truck body checking that the side door was locked and that the switch for the refrigeration plant was turned off. Normally, whenever they were running, whether empty or full, they kept the refrigeration going, but Seamus O'Brien had given him strict instructions. He walked away from the Saviem, turned right, out of the Fish Market, turned right again at the second turning and into the Kneipe three doors to the right, 'Der Goldene Anker', and ordered a beer. He had drunk half of it when the seat beside him was occupied. He could smell the perfume the man was wearing and glanced distastefully in the mirror at the long blond wavy hair, manicured and lacquered fingernails.

'Seamus didn't tell me what a great big masculine he-man you are,' Gorgeous George said.

'He probably didn't tell you that I can't stand poufters either,' Sam said. He took the spare bunch of keys belonging to Arthur Naylor out of his pocket. 'There you are,' he said, sliding them inconspicuously across the counter. 'Take them and piss off.'

'Ah Mmmmh, virile, aren't we?' George said. He reached into his pocket and produced a key, hanging from a large rubber ball. 'That's your room,' he said, 'upstairs on the second floor. It's bought and paid for. Better get an early night. Seamus wants you back at the truck at half past five. But if you're looking for something to do this evening . . .'

'I told you,' Sam said, 'piss off.'

The van had been parked next to a lorry, deep at the back of the Fish Market. The back doors of the van were opened and the side door of the truck gaped wide as a mouth, waiting to receive him. Here were few lights and the bright aluminium lining of the lorry revealed itself dimly. Regan climbed out of the back of the van, the skin of his neck prickling, the old tight feeling in his stomach. He used the step to climb into the back of the lorry and immediately the door slammed shut behind him. He saw the thickness of it, at least fifteen inches, and suddenly knew where the glass fibre Dr Furness had found in the Paki's lungs had come from. This was a refrigerated transport; the sides, behind the aluminium, would be fibre-glass and glass wool, both perfect insulators. He lurched forward into the depths of the truck, completely disorientated by the abrupt removal of light. He reached out his hand, felt his fingers touch the ice cold aluminium of the far wall. He put his back against the wall and stood perfectly still, holding his breath.

Whispers. Not voices – whispers of cloth on cloth, whispers of breathing, whispers of skin on material. Left. Right. Other side of the truck interior. A foot, slowly sliding across the aluminium floor. Regan silently crouched, turned so that his left side was against the wall. Lower down the sound was amplified, the slither of a leather sole, the faint but unmistakable clink of a loose toe-cap.

It has to come soon. While they still think they know. The breathing stops, count one, two, then a sudden exhalation, violent movement, grunts, clatter of feet. But no Regan. He'd dived along the floor away from the wall at an angle, using the wall to push himself off, not caring if his hands scraped. Roll over, come up in a line like an unwound spring, then stand still. They were slugging each other. Bloody amateurs. Regan cat-stepped in, listening for a grunt, then slammed the ram-rod of his arm forward, the flat of his palm smashing into the side of a skull. The man's head rocked and slammed against the aluminium wall but Regan was no longer there. He'd danced to the side, listened again, hardened a fist against his stomach and jabbed his elbow short and sharp sideways, feeling it sink into ribs.

Then up with his knee and sure enough a head and a face came down to meet it, gagging from the elbow jab, and Regan felt blood spatter on the fabric of his trousers. Turn round; really, just like fucking waltzing. He kicked out and his shoe located a knee and someone howled, but had the sense to shout. 'Back, lads, back into the corners.' Regan heard a hurried shuffle. How many? He counted three for sure. The corner behind him could be empty. Behind him and to his right. Move slowly. Somebody had taken charge. 'Harry?' he said. 'Here.' That put Harry left on the door side. 'Hans?' 'Here.' A German. Left, back of the truck. 'Friedrich?' 'Here.' Right, back of the truck. Whoever was doing the calling was speaking from a position somewhere near the middle of the truck. 'Right, you lot,' he said. 'Leave him to me. Nobody else move.'

He walked boldly across the truck, left of the door. Then started back, this time walking slowly and, from the noises he was making, weaving from side to side, covering the whole of the surface of the truck's inside. 'Right, you bastard,' he said, 'where are you?'

Regan ran into the corner deep inside the truck to the right of the door from where Friedrich had been waiting. It seemed as if Friedrich had spread his arms wide, one along each wall, Regan ran solid into the middle of him, brought up his knee, chopped right and left at where he estimated Friedrich's neck would be. Friedrich gave a ghastly moan, his breath rattled in his throat, his hands closed convulsively round Regan's back and then dropped away as Friedrich dropped, pole-axed. But Regan didn't wait to pick him up. He ran, quietly as possible while Friedrich was still sliding down, covering any sound Regan might make, into the corner to the right on the door side. Wrong, Regan, wrong. The man who'd been standing there hadn't answered the roll-call since his name had not been announced. He must have sensed Regan coming, and stepped slightly to the side. Regan brushed against the man's arm, tried to turn but too late. The man reached out, grabbed Regan's anorak jacket, and swung him sideways, like a pendulum, against the aluminium wall. Regan reeled, but the man had turned and kicked, and Regan's knee crumpled, his face whammed against the aluminium. He fought against losing consciousness, feeling the blood run down his cheek. The man shouted urgently, 'Keep back, I've got him down,' then kicked out, forward, the hard toe-cap of his boot slamming into Regan's spine. Regan's face went forward again, against the side, and star shells exploded inside his head. His hand touched the floor, slipped in what he sensed was blood from his streaming nose. Another kick, and now his back felt broken, and a pain which began in his spine rushed upwards and exploded in his mind like a mushroom cloud, floating him away to eternity.

When he came round he was lying flat on his back, staring into the overhead light of the truck. Seamus O'Brien was sitting on the floor, his back to the unpainted aluminium wall. Regan sat upright, pain stabbing his lower back, and slowly dragged himself until he could rest against a wall. Four men in the back of the truck, two looking as if a steam roller had run over them. He grunted with satisfaction. At least, he'd achieved something.

' 'Tis a hard man you are, Mr Chafferty,' Seamus said. 'I thought the four of them would be enough for you, but apparently, they wasn't.'

Regan grunted, feeling his face which was caked with dried blood. He took out his handkerchief and blew his nose, staining the cotton red. Gently he explored his cheeks and his nose, wincing when his fingers found the bruises and lacerations. 'Fine travel courier you are,' he said to Seamus O'Brien, 'Clarkson Tours was never like this.'

Seamus chuckled. 'A fine sense of humour, Mr Chafferty, is a boon to any man. And an agreeable way to end one's days on this earth. You see, you made just one little mistake. That telephone in your girlfriend's apartment. Now explain to me, Mr Chafferty, why it is that me, with all my contacts here in the *Postamt* in Hamburg, all my friends that from time to time I oblige in one way or another, just explain to me how it was I wasn't able to put an address on to that telephone number. It was a '*Sonder*' number – know what that means, Mr Chafferty? *Special.* Not for the eyes of ordinary mortals like me. Now would you explain to me exactly how you, a fugitive from what is usually and laughably called justice, come to rate a telephone in the *Sonders* file? Just who are you, Mr Chafferty? That's what we're all most anxious to find out. And to save time, we're going to give you the chance to tell us, aren't we, lads?'

The 'lads' had moved forward. Regan heard again the ominous jingle of that loose toe-cap and, though his muscles tightened by reflex action, he knew that any resistance would be hopeless.

Fuck Ingrid and her special telephone. Damn, blast, and sod the *Sonder* telephone files. He looked up at the four men, and when he spoke, his voice was that of the Regan of the Sweeney, the tough cop who takes no crap from any man. 'You lot,' he said, 'Piss off out of it. I want a word in private with O'Brien here. And I don't want your elephant ears flapping around while I do it.'

They looked at Seamus O'Brien, totally bemused.

'What the hell,' Regan said, 'he's got his pea-shooter and he's a big boy now.'

Seamus gave a long low chuckle that seemed to start from somewhere in his bowels and swelled up to burst out of him. He wiped the laughter tears away from his eyes with his handkerchief, and did the Dan Maskell bit with the Mauser. 'What a character you are, Mr Chafferty, to be sure,' he said. 'All right, boys. Do as he says. Anyway, you've things to do out there.'

The four men left the back of the truck. Seamus O'Brien watched them go, but the gun in his hand never wavered. A 7.65 bullet may be small, but it will still do all the damage needed in he right place. And this gun, Regan knew, was aimed at the right place.

'Right,' Seamus said when the door had been closed tight again, 'You were going to tell me a fairy story?'

'I was going to do a deal.'

'A deal, is it. Forgive me asking, but what with? I have

always understood that a deal is between two people, each of whom possess something the other needs. I don't think you understand, Mr Chafferty, if that truly is your name. You have nothing I *need*. The information we were about to extract from you isn't important to us, you know. Merely a diversion. So far as I'm concerned, you're already dead. I have a neat and tidy organization that pays good money. I don't get a pension at the end of it, but that doesn't matter. I'm not about to take any risks, Mr Chafferty, and the moment I discovered that you had a *Sonder* telephone number, I knew you could be a risk to me. You're dead, Mr Chafferty, and dead men don't make deals.'

'Why do you think I was in Hamburg?' Regan said quietly.

'I don't know, Mr Chafferty and frankly, it would be too expensive and too risky for me to find out.'

'Why do you think I want to go to England, this route?'

'Because, being wanted by Interpol, you couldn't go any other way.'

Regan laughed, trying desperately to make it sound convincing.

'For ten thousand deutschmarks, I could have bought a berth on any one of a hundred tramp steamers going to any one of a hundred destinations. You boast about being a pro, O'Brien, but for my money, you're just a pumped-up barrel of shit. Look at that fucking Mauser. A 7.65. You're vain, O'Brien, so vain you want to boast about your marksmanship. Well this isn't Bisley, you great fat git, it's the real thing. If you're going to carry a gun – and that makes you an A.1. cunt in any language – you want a stopper, a bloody shooting iron that fires a slug so big you don't have to aim it. A .45 Colt – now there's a gun.'

Regan's hand was resting on his knee. The gun spat, and the sound of it reverberated around the aluminium interior like a land-mine. When Regan looked down, he saw a long furrow in the fleshy part of his hand between his thumb and forefinger, where the shot had neatly scooped a channel an eighth of an inch deep. The blood was already starting to well up from the bottom of the channel but, as yet, he could feel no pain. That, he knew, would come later.

'That could have been your testicle,' Seamus O'Brien said. 'Now cut out the insults and start to say something with a bit of meaning in it. Why *were* you here in Hamburg? And why *were* you going to England, this route? You'll notice I already use the past tense so far as you're concerned.'

'I am here in Hamburg to plan a job. I am going to England this route to test it. If it's a safe route, I shall bring a specialist back with me, this way.'

At the mention of a job, Seamus O'Brien's eyes had opened wide. 'A job, is it? No doubt a big one?'

'The biggest.' Regan was thinking hard. What was it that Ingrid had said, just one item in the many police items they'd gossiped about, shop talking the way any two people in the same trade will do when they are necessarily cooped up together. Something to do with the Post Office . . .? He ransacked his memory to try to pull back the details, but all he could remember was the fierce passion of Ingrid's love-making, the way that every moment of being with her had been charged with a high-tension awareness of their mutual sexuality.

'Hang on a minute,' he temporized. 'You said a deal can come about when each of the two parties have something the other one wants . . .'

'Not *wants*. Needs!' Seamus O'Brien said.

'I prefer wants. What's happened here has taught me that you have an organization with a lot of good heavy muscle. My job could use that. Shit, I don't need it. I can bring in my own muscle. But it makes economic sense for me to use yours.'

'Now you're talking like an accountant,' Seamus O'Brien said, 'and like all of that mean snivelling horrible bunch of fakers, you're not comitting yourself to any details.'

It came back to Regan in a flash. Special Police Escort for a truck carrying the Post Office money. One truck made the trip during the night, all round Hamburg, came back into the Huehnerposten every morning with a fortune on board. Ingrid's boss had been asked to infiltrate a few unknown plain clothes people to carry out one of their periodic security checks. Very much against her wishes, Ingrid had been assigned to it with Olga.

She'd given him the details. The danger times were Fridays, especially when that day fell at the beginning of a month. 'Five million deutschmarks in used notes. I know where I can pick it up any time I like. It needs muscle.'

'And this specialist you were going to bring from England?'

'The fastest jelly man in the business.'

'It's a safe? Safe jobs are out of fashion. Too much money to be made in the con game these days.'

'I never said it was a safe.'

'Now you wouldn't be bringing in a jelly man just to open a can of sardines, would you? And you wouldn't be needing a special telephone with a Sondernummer to phone up a canning factory, would you? You've got a big mouth, Chafferty, but when you open it and wobble your lips about nothing comes out of any substance or value.'

'Telephones are installed by the Post Office. The Post Office also has other departments. One of them receives and pays out a considerable amount of money. The man who got me that Sonder telephone can also help me get that money.'

Seamus slowly put the gun back into his pocket. He was chuckling. 'Knocking over the Post Office. What an immoral fellow you are, to be sure, and what terrible problems you give me, to be sure.'

'Problems?'

'Yes. I'm wondering how the devil I'm going to spend my half of five million deutschmarks. I take it you was meaning to share and share alike, now wasn't you?'

'Heads, you win, tails, I lose,' Regan said.

'Exactly. Now we better get you on your way to England, hadn't we? I wouldn't want you to keep the fastest jelly man in the business waiting! What's more, I wouldn't want you to be missing the Changing of the Guard.'

Ingrid and Olga and a bewildered Detective Sergeant Carter were having a consultation in Ingrid's apartment. 'I saw him come out of the shop, I watched the contact being made! They walked together to the corner and then they disappeared. Bugger it, I was already moving when they got to the corner. If it wasn't for that bloody Volkswagen tried to cut me off as I was pulling out ...! I only had my eyes off them for ten seconds.'

'If only he'd woken me up before he left,' Ingrid said. 'Damn him! We had twenty people all ready to go with one phone call from me. Five cars. Two police marine patrol boats, a helicopter, and the stubborn mule just walked straight into the middle of it. If only ...'

Olga's hand slammed on the table. 'If only you two would stop saying "if only",' she thundered in heavily accented English. 'We must all think what shall we now do? Obviously, all boats leaving the harbour must be searched from side to side!'

'From top to bottom, you mean,' Ingrid said.

'Side to side, top to bottom, what does it matter? They must not be allowed to leave Hamburg with the inspector. Now we must throw the net around them and squeeze them tight like pips from the orange.'

Ingrid looked at Carter with raised eyebrows. 'Four weeks at Berlitz and she thinks she's Jane Eyre. Shut up Olga, let me think.' Carter stood up and walked to the window. He looked out moodily then turned back round to them.

'I hate like hell to say this,' he said, 'but I don't think, to use Olga's phrase, we should throw that net anywhere, or else, again to quote Olga, I think the guvnor might wind up being the pip that gets squeezed. You don't know Jack Regan, and I do! He's a loner. A law to himself. Wherever he is he'll be using his loaf ...'

'Using his loaf?' Olga said. 'This is no time for supper!'

'Leave it,' Ingrid said, 'Halt den Mund.'

'The Chef Inspektor won't like it,' she said. 'We've got the whole thing set up. There'll be hell to pay!'

'Look,' Carter said, 'you want the Tiger, right? To get the Tiger we have to get the network that brings him in and out. The network itself doesn't mean a bloody thing, in fact I can see what the guvnor is thinking. It might be worth both our whiles to keep that network open and just siphon off the passengers whenever we want to.'

'You mean, just let them go ahead and smuggle Regan out of the country?'

'That's exactly what I mean.'

Ingrid thought about it for a moment, then she and Olga had a rapid exchange in Plattdeutsch, rightly guessing that Carter with his A-level Hochdeutsch wouldn't be able to follow them. He got some of it, words like *your responsibility*, *fired*, *problems*, but not very much else. 'What are *you* going to do?' she asked Carter.

'I'm going to take a chance and be on that *Prinz Hamlet* when she pulls out in the morning. Anyway, I've got some torn-up deutschmarks! I wouldn't like to see Regan dropped into the tom-tit because I've got the bees and honey in my sky.'

'Tom-tit, bees and honey? Olga said. 'It's back to Berlitz for me.'

Regan got the special treatment. He was taken in the back of the van to the 'Café Tangier'. The Moroccan decorations, the dim lights, looked as if they had been bought at Woolworth's. Behind the café was a two storey apartment with a door leading into a network of back alleys. Upstairs were three bedrooms and an office.

'I use this place sometimes,' Seamus O'Brien said, 'when I'm indulging myself in an affair of the heart. You know how it is. Man does not live by bread alone.' As if to demonstrate his words the waiter from the café brought in a tray of steaming hot tea and a bottle of white wine. 'Usually we serve beer,' Seamus O'Brien said, 'but I can't stand the stuff the way the Germans make it,' he said. 'It's only one kind I like; the Maibock as they call it. But you can't get it too often; in fact the silly buggers only make it once a year.'

'The wine will be fine,' Regan said.

A tall, thin, cadaverous man came in when they had finished supper, smelling of mothballs, ether and piss. He took one look at Regan's face and his hand, opened the black bag he carried, sprinkled liquid from a bottle on to a piece of near white rag and sponged Regan's cuts. Regan grimaced when the almost raw alcohol bit into him. The man looked at the wound on Regan's hand and clucked. He manipulated the skin roughly on either side of it and caused the blood to flow again. Regan groaned. But the man ignored him and wiped away the congealed and the new blood with the other side of the rag covered in the same liquid. Regan could have screamed, but he saw Seamus O'Brien's eye on him. The man opened a box which contained a large powder puff and what looked like talcum. He dabbed it all over Regan's face and his hand and Seamus O'Brien chuckled. ''Tis beautiful you are,' he said. The man put the powder puff away and snapped his bag and then, without having said a single word since he arrived, turned and left.

'I suppose he's going back to the butcher's shop,' Regan said. But Seamus held up a finger. 'You cannot judge by appearances, Mr Chafferty,' he said. 'That man used to be a brilliant brain surgeon in Dresden. Know what that means?'

'I can guess,' Regan said. 'He got his stethoscope caught in the Iron Curtain. Or was it a bottle?' He couldn't feel his wounds any more. He went to bed, stripped, climbed under the feather duvet and slept like a baby.

They woke him an hour before dawn. There was no sign of Seamus O'Brien, but the waiter brought him coffee and a plastic shopping bag. 'Essen,' he said. 'Food for the voyage. Now come quick.'

The black van was waiting in one of the back alleys with the same driver and this time Regan sat in the front passenger seat. 'Nice night,' he said.

'Shut up.'

That was the sum total of dialogue that passed between them as they made their way back to the Fish Market, and into the back of the aluminium lined truck, where twenty obvious Pakistanis were waiting, sitting around the walls in yoga-like positions of patience, resignation, and determination. This wasn't the first place they'd waited on their long voyage from the poverty of Pakistan to the incomprehensible wealth of the white man's welfare state. The door slammed and was locked from the outside. Almost immediately the lorry pulled away. Regan, seeing all wall space occupied, sat down with his back to the door. After five minutes the lorry pulled up again and they waited. In the gleam of the overhead lamp which had been left alight, Regan looked at the faces round the wall seeing here and there the gleams of hope, eager expectation that overlay the centuries of deprivation, disease and despair. 'It's got nothing to do with me,' he told himself. 'My job is the administration of the fucking law!' The law said very specific things about travelling into England with or without a passport. He longed to put out his hand and say to the first man 'Look, it's got nothing to do with me, so far as I'm concerned you can all come and go as you please!'

On this whole question of blacks and whites, of immigrants and residents, Enoch Powell versus the whole racial prejudice bit, Regan was absolutely neutral. He divided the world in his own way, villains versus the rest. The colour of a man's face, the church to which he went or didn't go, the kind of politics he voted had not the slightest effect. A villain was a villain, nothing else, and a non-villain was a non-villain. These men weren't villains, they were the victims of buggers like Seamus O'Brien. Every one of them doubtless had pledged ninety per cent of his income during the next ten years to pay back the cost of this trip. The minute they arrived a way would be found for them to assume an identity; they'd be given some kind of identity documents that would let them sign on for unemployment and any other benefit that might be going. They'd live in sub-human slum conditions in Brixton, Birmingham, Manchester, or Cardiff, twenty to a room by day another twenty in the same six feet by two feet spaces at night. And nine tenths of all the money that came their way would go through the sticky hands of their brothers, the final mesh in a cog of misery that went all the way back to the sunny, stinking, starving villages from which they had come. Regan opened his plastic bag, tore the paper wrappings of the packages it contained with anger, pulled out the thick slices of brown bread, the boiled ham, sausages, the cheese, and offered them round. The nearest man looked at the boiled ham and shook his head. He reached into the pocket of his cheap suit and pulled out a handful of maize grains.

When he spoke, his voice was soft and melodiously cultured. 'I am not wishing to give you offence, sir,' he said, 'but I am afraid we are not eating your kind of food. Our religion, you see, forbids the consumption of the flesh of animals. Would you, sir, do me the honour of accepting my grains. You will find them wholesome and nourishing.'

Regan looked at the mess he had spread out. The ham made of the flesh of pigs, the wurst made from blood, the butter from milk from the udder of a cow and suddenly he felt a raising wave of nausea and self-disgust. Without bothering to rewrap it he stuffed the whole lot back into the plastic bag, reached out, took one of the maize grains put it between his teeth and cracked it.

'Good appetite, sir,' the Pakistani said, smiling kindly at him.

Sam Little stopped the Saviem at the end of the line of trucks on the embarkation parking lot. A little fat man came running across the tarmac at him. Sam opened his door and waited. 'Morning Sam,' the little man said, bustling with officialdom and self-importance. 'You're late,' he said. 'You usually get in the night before. I was saving a place for you up at the front. But I had to let it go. I've done what paperwork I can.'

'You worry too much, Andreas,' Sam said. 'There's plenty of time. Damn thing doesn't leave until midday.' He handed the wallet of papers to Andreas, Pat Booth's shipping agent in Hamburg.

'Do you want me to check the back?' Andreas said.

Sam felt a brief flare of panic. 'You don't need to,' he said. 'We came empty out of Innsbruck.'

'You know I should check,' Andreas said. 'You men are so careless. Remember the time when Peter came through and said he was empty and it turned out they'd left a whole box of car parts in there. You know I have to certify as the agent that you're travelling empty. It's my neck, you know.'

'You're being too Germanic,' Sam said, knowing that for some odd reason Andreas's great pride was in being mistaken for an English gentleman. He even bought a bowler hat every time he came to England, whenever he attended an agents' conference. The drivers teased him and called him 'My lord'.

'I am *not* being Germanic, I'm merely trying to be efficient.'

He turned on his heel and minced away towards the Immigration and customs. Sam smiled with relief when he saw him go. No doubt about it, Andreas *was* efficient, possibly the most efficient agent they had. Nobody ever had any trouble coming into or out of Hamburg, which was doubtless why Seamus O'Brien had picked Booth's run through that port.

As soon as Andreas had gone, Sam got out of the cab and went to the side door of the truck body. He unlocked it, opened it a fraction and waited for a moment or two, following the instructions Seamus had given him back in England. His hands were sweating and he felt the water running down his body from under his armpits and between his legs. 'Well, get it over with,' he told himself and opened the door just wide enough to get his body through. They'd obviously been instructed well when they were loaded on board and all were pressed into the corners on the door side where they couldn't be seen by anyone looking casually in. He felt nervous and embarrassed and that made his manner brusque.

'I'll say what I've got to say in English,' he said, 'and if anybody doesn't understand then somebody else had better translate it for him. But wait until I finish. You've all been given one of these,' he said, holding up a piece of metal shaped like a T with a shank about two inches long the end of which had been hammered square. He walked to one of the panels that lined the truck wall, located the four square slots, put the key in each one and turned it. When he had unfastened the last one the panel came away from the wall revealing a space lined with aluminium, set between the fibreglass insulation which showed at the top and the bottom.

He looked at Regan. 'Do you understand English,' he said. Regan nodded. 'Right,' he said, 'you can give a demonstration. What you do is get into that space. See this handle. When you're inside pull this panel towards you and hold on to that handle. Got the idea?' Regan nodded again, climbed into the space, grasped the handle and pulled it. When he had done so Sam put his key into the four slots and locked the panel, which fitted neatly into position. No-one could have told that a man was hiding there. Sam Little unlocked the panel again and Regan stepped out. 'Now this is what you do,' Sam said, 'and listen carefully. Every time the truck stops I want you all to get into these holes. 'You,' he said to Regan, 'lock everybody in. Then you get in yourself and hold your panel shut. If I'm the first man into the back of the truck I will lock off your panel. But if for any reason I'm not the first man in or there is anybody watching me I rely on you to hold that panel tight. Do you get me?'

'Yes,' Regan said, 'I get you. But why have we all been given a key, if I'm the only one who is going to use it?'

'If you look up in that corner,' Sam said, 'you'll find there's a hooter. If I blow that hooter I shall want you all in quickly. There wouldn't be time for you to lock them all without help.'

'That makes sense,' Regan said.

Sam looked at him. 'You're British, aren't you?' he said. 'What the hell are you doing smuggling yourself into Britain?'

'I'm behind with my alimony,' Regan said. 'My wife's lawyers are looking for me.' It was the fastest thing he could think of, but he could see Sam wasn't convinced. 'Look,' he said, 'you drive the truck and I'll hold on to the door. How does that grab you?'

'I get the point,' Sam said, 'sorry I opened my big mouth.'

The lorry moved forward and, after fifty yards or so, it stopped again. By the time Sam Little had climbed into the back, the passengers were all locked away. He rapped on the panel of the box containing Jack Regan. 'Good going,' he said. 'Now, I'm afraid you'll have to stay in there until we're on board.' Regan shuddered as he heard the four catches slide home, totally imprisoning him. The box in which he was encased, standing upright with his arms by his side, gave him no room to turn around, or to bend down, or even, he suddenly realized, to lift his hands to scratch a tickle on his face. And of course, no doubt psychosomatically, his face immediately began to itch, as if ants were trekking across it. He leaned his forehead forward until it touched the cool aluminium side and allowed his whole weight to sag down. He couldn't get out of his mind the image of all those dead men on their slabs, the aluminium traces beneath their finger-nails. When he'd entered the box the first time, he'd immediately seen the signs he'd looked in vain for in Booth's yard. No wonder the cleaners hadn't seen them. Doubtless neither the cleaners nor any one else at Booths, except the drivers, knew anything about the illicit shipments. One anomaly struck him; Sam Little had seemed incredibly nervous when he'd briefed them all, as if he were doing it for the first time. Of course, if he was the man who'd failed to unlock the men Regan had seen in the morgue at Bletchley, the man who'd spent half a night weighting them with slabs and floating them out on the water, then he had a lot to be nervous about. Regan had an instinct, a nose, and it told him that Sam Little wasn't the right type for this job. He didn't smell like a hardened villain, a man who'd be prepared to dump all those corpses into the reservoir. Criminals have an experience or an innocence and any copper worth his salt can tell the difference a mile away. How many lads had Regan clipped around the ear and told — 'Piss off home to your Mum, you're out of your depth here . . .'

And how many times had Regan said, 'Yeah, yeah!' when an obvious old lag had said – 'let me go. I've never done such a thing before and I'll never do it again.' And then snapped the cuffs round his wrist.

God, even though the aluminium was cold to the touch, he was sweating. And scared. More scared than he'd ever admit. What a rotten way this would be to die. In his sudden panic he felt as if he couldn't breathe, as if already the air in the box had been exhausted, replaced with pure carbon dioxide. He panicked and tried holding his breath, held it as long as he could then cursed himself when the long gasp came from him and he had to inhale again, deep, taking in a full lung. Jesus, that wasn't the way to survive. Shallow breathing, little bit, quick in, hold it briefly, quick out, like panting. That was the way to conserve air, wasn't it, not this deep in, deep out routine.

The truck was moving again. Stopping. Starting, stopping. The sound of a hand slapping the outside reverberated through his skull. He heard the international 'okay'. The truck started again, clanked over metal grids, went down a hill where all sounds reverberated, then stopped. Thank God. They were on the ferry.

Hildegarde Zustein shifted her arm gently, pulling it from beneath Arthur Naylor's neck. He was lying flat on his back, snoring. She reached on to the bedside table for a cigarette, lighting it quietly with the lighter Pieter Varenk had given her. She smiled when she thought of Pieter. No-one would ever accuse him of being handsome but, by God, there was a man. If only she'd met him four years ago and not that bastard Willi, who messed her about, got her pregnant, and then didn't want to know her. And then, if only she hadn't met that blasted Irishman, who'd introduced her to Seamus O'Brien, who'd offered to get her to one of the newly-legal abortion clinics in England, if she was prepared to pay the price. She didn't have money. Willi, the bastard, had seen to that, and when Seamus suggested 'services' she thought he was another little fat dirty middle-aged man, wanting to get his hand up her skirt and lacking the guts to do it the normal way. Well, it had been almost that way, hadn't it. This stinking bugger, Arthur

Naylor, whose clothes, whose skin even, always smelled of diesel-oil and car-grease. Who had dirty fingernails. Who snored. She shifted in bed angrily and Arthur half woke. She slipped quickly out of the bed; he was always horny when he woke up and now she'd got to the stage when even touching him made her flesh crawl. And then the tickets. Those blasted tickets, she thought, as she stepped under the shower. She'd been a damned fool to agree with that, in addition to sleeping with the guy. Because fiddling the flight tickets for Arthur Naylor the way she had, put her outside the law. If the airline got to know about that, she'd be prosecuted, lose her job, no doubt go to prison. She couldn't even plead first offence, since she'd done it several times now, and Seamus was likely to have arranged to keep the stubs.

What would happen with Pieter if she went inside for a few months? Curtains to that love affair. And she wanted, so desperately, to keep him, if only she could. God, if only she could. No more Arthur Naylors. No more fiddling one-way tickets, Hamburg to Gatwick, on the charter lines. No more stink of diesel fuel, and waking up with the sound of that bloody awful snoring in her ears, and those dirty fingernails on her shoulder. She dried herself, pulled on her dressing-gown and sat by the phone in the living-room of her flat. She dialled the number Seamus had given her. A voice answered and she identified herself. The voice said. He's not here. We'll have to call you back. Is everything all right? Yes, yes, everything was all right. She put the phone down, tears springing to her eyes. Sod it. She'd screwed her courage to the point at which she could have told Seamus O'Brien to stick it. And he wasn't there. She felt deflated as a balloon after a party. If only she had the guts to risk it and tell Pieter when he came in on his next flight. He'd work out a way to deal with it. But Pieter was out of Hamburg on the New York run and wouldn't be back for two days. Bloody hell. She bent her head and tears ran unchecked down her cheek. The door to the bedroom opened and Arthur Naylor stood there, uncovered, a damn great stalk like a sunflower sticking out of his middle.

'Where are you love,' he said plaintively, 'I've got a present for you.'

'And I've got a fucking present for you,' she shouted, leaped to her feet, seized the jar of water and cut flowers from the shelf, and threw it at him. It smashed into his middle, broke, and showered his cock with stalks, pot shards and water. 'You needed a fucking bath, you dirty bastard,' she shouted, then went for him with her nails unsheathed like a cat's claws.

The sandy-haired Immigration Officer on the Irish Desk at Heathrow fingered a new moustache he was in the process of growing, thinking about Mavis and the way she'd reacted when he'd started to grow it. Now she'd come round to his way of thinking. It made him *look* older and, in his job, that was important. He was so busy thinking about Mavis and their visit last evening to the lighted windows of the cut-price furniture shop in the High Street at Ealing Common that, when he saw the photograph of Seamus O'Brien staring at him out of the proffered passport, and lifted his head to compare it to the face, he remembered at once the photograph he'd inspected in the Duty Room, but forgot in which category the photograph had been placed. Was this man a VIP who had to be hurried through? A Member of Parliament to be called sir and speeded on his way? Or a villain, to be held in irons to await the tumbril to the Tower? Oh dear. He looked at Seamus's face. No help there! He checked the list beside his desk by swivelling his eyes. No help there, either! 'Would you mind waiting a minute, sir,' he said, modulating his voice the way the speech therapist had taught him. He stepped back, reached for the telephone, heard the immediate click at the other end. 'Seamus O'Brien,' he whispered, 'He was on the board this morning. I'm holding him. Shall I ring the alarm?'

'You berk! He's Category D, and in case you've forgotten, that means, note movements for file, but do not interfere . . .'

He put down the telephone as if it were hot. 'Ringing up your bookie, was you?' Seamus asked.

The Immigration Officer stroked his moustache nervously as he handed the passport to Seamus O'Brien, Category D. 'Something like that,' he said.

Regan could hear the voices echoing outside the truck, the sounds of engines roaring, the boom of men's feet on the steel interior catwalks and companionways. 'Bloody hell, why doesn't he come and let us out,' he grumbled. Now he could taste the monoxide air of the car exhausts, and in his imagination, felt his throat constrict. 'Damn it, we're going to choke to death,' he said. Every muscle in his body ached from even that small amount of time spent standing and immobile. Then he heard the side door of the truck open and hope was renewed, and dashed when it became apparent that Sam Little was releasing the others first, working his way anti-clockwise round the interior.

At last, it came to Regan's turn. He almost fell out of the coffin, reached up and yanked his tie loose and his shirt neck open. 'I thought I was a goner,' he said.

'The first ten thousand miles is the worst,' Sam Little said, hoping to cheer him. He gathered them all round him and started to talk quietly. 'You'll have to stay down here,' he said, 'during the voyage. I'm told there'll be nobody on this deck at all, which will be locked as soon as the boat sails. There's a lavatory in the corner that you can use, but one of you must keep on watch all the time. Understand? If anybody spots any one of you, I shall deny I know anything about you and let them arrest you as stowaways. Get that quite clear. I shall do nothing to help any man foolish enough to let himself be seen. As soon as you hear the sailors start moving about tomorrow morning, all get back into the truck, shut the door, and wait there until I come. Understand?' They all nodded. Regan looked round the circle and suddenly felt a shock run through him. The man in the row in front of him. To the left. Where his collar had rubbed against the edge of his cheek when he had sweated in the box, the brown colour had started to rub away. Exposing white flesh beneath. Regan could have cursed. So many brown faces, all clustered together. Of course, you don't look at each one individually! But he, Regan, should have. Now he came to look at the back of the man's hair, he could see the difference. The other men's hair was naturally dark blue-black and shiny. This man's hair had been slicked down and brilliantined flat, probably even dyed that blue-black colour. Apart from that, he seem indistinguishable from the others at first glance. No doubt a study of his features, which Regan couldn't see at the moment, would give him away. But who looked at individual features in such a crowd. Regan knew he had made the same error a lot of people make; he'd expected to see Pakistanis, had preformed an image of his travelling companions, and when he'd been confronted by all those brown faces, he'd accepted them all.

Sam Little went over his instructions once more then looked directly at Regan in the back row. 'You,' he said, 'I'm putting you in charge down here. Make sure that if anybody goes to the lavatory, somebody else is on watch. Make sure that nobody messes about on this level. Above all, remember that the fate of all of you depends on each and every one of you.' Regan felt like giving him the Boy Scout signal, and the Ra-Ra-Ra, but didn't speak. When Sam Little addressed him directly, every head had swivelled in his direction. Except one.

Now, why could that be? Regan asked himself.

It was sheer coincidence that Charlie Smythe, one of the Customs Officers on duty in the Green (nothing to declare) Channel had just finished reading yet another book on Occupational Psychology, and a popular newspaper article on Body Language, both of which told him not to look at a man's face to read his mind, but at his feet, his hands, the set of his shoulders, the way in which he carried himself, the position he took up in a room vis-à-vis its other occupants. When Seamus O'Brien turned the corner committing himself to the Green Channel, his briefcase bumped into a woman who'd stopped there, no doubt frightened by the ack-ack barrage of Officer's eyes.

Seamus, basically courteous though a complete villain, stepped back to permit the woman to make up her mind whether to proceed or not. He waved his arm with an old-fashioned sweep. 'After you, my dear,' he said. Again she hesitated. Again the sweep of the hand. No, the woman had decided against proceeding. Seamus gave her a smile, looked at the officers to reassure her and smiled again. No, she'd suddenly remembered a half a bottle of eau-de-cologne she'd better let them examine and for that she'd need to pass through the Red Channel. Seamus hitched up his trousers, shot his cuffs. 'Ah, well,' inclination of his left shoulder, 'she knew best.' Turn around, smile again, and walk forward. This illustrated catalogue of waves, nods, winks, smiles, and gestures, that would have done the conductor of a Beethoven Symphony proud was a whole lexicon of meaning to Charlie Smythe. *He* raised *his* hand and his immaculate body language said imperiously. 'You! Come 'ere!'

A half an hour and a body and orifice search later, he was reluctantly compelled to wave Seamus O'Brien a sad goodbye. Seamus gave him a sign that anywhere could have been read as, 'up yours, mate'.

Detective Sergeant Carter went aboard the *Prinz Hamlet* at half past eleven. As plain Mr Carter, he'd booked an outside single berth cabin, but had compromised by having a shower instead of a bath. There'd be hell enough to pay when he put in his expenses, especially if Regan was on the same boat with no bed to sleep in.

He threw his small suitcase on the bed, locked the cabin behind him, and walked up to the promenade deck, from which he could look down on the other embarking passengers. Though it was early in the season the boat appeared to be full and a continuous file of passengers streamed up the gangplank, while a steady line of cars, vans, and lorries, drove over the ramp into the stern. Most of the passengers carried large suitcases which they held easily, as if empty. Carter had no doubt they'd be loaded on the return voyage with the spoils of a cut-price Britain. Carter felt insult added to the injury when he saw the number of new cars being pushed aboard, all still covered with the protective wax direct from the factories of West Germany, the Porsches, Mercedes, Opels, Volkswagens, BMWs, part of the forty-five per cent of imported cars with which the suicidal British kamikaze their own car industry.

And then his patriotism burst back into flower when he saw the black rolls pull up alongside the gangplank. It seemed to him to have a distinguished and superior air. He turned to his neighbour at the rail. 'Good car that,' he said. 'A Rolls Royce! They make them in Derby, England, you know!'

'Wie, bitte?' the man asked puzzled.

Carter shrugged, pointed to the car.

'Ein schoenes Auto,' the man said, beaming. 'Mercedes, nicht wahr?'

The man sitting next to the chauffeur, wearing a dark suit, a Homburg hat and tinted spectacles, leaped out of the front of the car, and opened the back door. He reached inside and helped out a frail old lady, wearing all black with a black hat and veil. The burly man, some sort of personal servant, held the frail old lady's arm and assisted her along the pontoon beside which the boat was moored, then up the steep gangplank, mounting slowly, side by side.

The man beside Carter had taken off his hat and stood with it held across his chest. Carter himself felt like saluting and blowing a pipe as they arrived at the boat-side and the streaming crowds parted like the waters of Jordan.

The Chief Steward hurried forward; the servant held out the ticket; the Chief Steward read it and almost ruptured himself with his bow. 'Would you please be so good as to follow me, your ladyship?' he said, then led the way towards the de luxe cabin area.

Carter stared after the servant; that was the second time he had mistaken her for a man!

The Pakistanis showed little inclination to leave the back of the truck, but squatted yoga style in one corner all herded together. It couldn't have been for warmth since the steampipes which ran through the car deck kept the interior at a constant temperature. Regan opened the door cautiously and looked out. As Sam Little had said, the car deck was deserted. The doors to the upper decks all shut. Lacking the discipline of the East he felt a need to go to the lavatory. He beckoned to the man whose cheek he'd seen rubbed white, who was sitting at the edge of the group of Pakistanis.

'I'm going to the lavatory,' Regan said, 'come and stand outside the door and let me know if anyone comes.' The man nodded. Regan stared into his face. 'You understand me,' Regan said and the man nodded again.

Slowly and carefully they made their way between the parked lorries and vans. To the side of the inner shaft. Regan checked the off-side door of a nearby van; a careless driver had left it unlocked. 'If you see or hear one of those bulkhead doors start to open,' Regan said, 'knock on the lavatory door and then get into the van. I'll stay in here until whoever it is has gone.'

No knock came on the door and Regan and the man eventually went back to the truck. The Pakistanis were still sitting crosslegged in the group in the corner and the man went to join them while Regan sat on the step of the truck with the door partly open, watching the car deck, thinking. In his mind he was washing the cocoa-make-up off that man's face. He was shampooing the grease out of the man's hair, blow-drying it and doing a teasy-weazy sit-up-and-beg job on him. And then he was remembering the film show he had seen in London arranged by courtesy of Immigration; he was seeing the plinth of the base of Nelson's Column in Trafalgar Square, the crudely handled but still effective zoom-in shot taken from the roof of the National Gallery, the wobbly but still recognizable full-face close-up of the man they called the Tiger.

Carter found Sam Little in the cafeteria and put himself in the queue. The photograph Miss Pringle had given him was an unusual likeness. He noticed that Sam Little avoided the German Wurst, Scholle, Sauerbraten, Eisbein exotica and settled for a conventional Fish with Chips, even asking for and getting a helping of peas. Carter heard him ask for tomato ketchup. The man behind the counter – no doubt a Gastarbeiter Phillipino – smiled, reached below the counter and handed Sam Little not one, but six plastic cachets each of which appeared to contain a sample of blood. Carter chose the Scholle, a plump flat fish, grilled in butter with plain boiled potatoes – the last thing he wanted to risk was a pain in his gut that demanded trips to the lavatory. He took his meal and sat at the same table as Sam Little, remembering one of Regan's first rules of surveillance. 'If you can't avoid your subject seeing you get as close to him as you can. That way you destroy suspicion before it even begins. It's the man twelve or fifteen feet away with probing eyes that a suspect becomes aware of; you rarely believe that the man sitting opposite you, talking openly to you is in fact shadowing you!' He looked openly at Sam Little's plate, watched him open every one of the tomato sauce cachets and flood his food with them.

'You need tomato sauce to give this foreign muck a bit of taste,' Sam Little said defensively. He eyed Carter's plate, looked up at his face, mistaking him for a German. 'Don't get me wrong, I mean no offence, it's, like, what you're used to, isn't it?'

'Ja,' Carter said flexing his A-level muscles.

'You understand English then, do you? I don't talk German.'

'I ought to,' Carter said, 'I am English.'

'Yeh, well, I thought for a moment you was, like, German.'

From where he was sitting, Carter had seen Olga in the queue. Of the little old lady there was no sign. Olga gave a visible sign of recognizing Carter when she had collected her plate of Wurst und Sauerkraut. Carter groaned inwardly. She prowled heavy footed across the cafeteria towards him, stood at the end of the table beaming down at him. They don't teach you, in the A-level, the German for piss off but Carter did his best.

'Geh weg,' he said, 'dieser Mann ist der Fahrer,' praying that Sam Little had not lied when he said he couldn't speak German. Olga muttered something not even Carter could understand and went to sit at a table on the other side of the cafeteria.

'Funny looking bloke,' Sam Little said, 'do you know him?'

'Not particularly . . .'

'He looks a bit queer to me.'

'That's why I don't know him. He tried to pick me up.'

'Very wise. They get up to some funny things, them queers.'

'Yes, don't they?'

Though he couldn't know it, Carter had the same reaction Regan had had to Sam Little. Either the driver was a superb actor, or he was too naïve to be a hardened criminal, the partner in a multi-thousand pound body smuggling racket. Of course, he could be a tool, a man being used without his knowledge, but Carter doubted that. One thing was certain; if he was a villain, he was missing his vocation. He ought to have been on television or the stage with an act like that. He was entirely typical of a working class chauvinistic insular Englishman, with two weeks holiday in Majorca or the Costa Brava, two weeks spent pining for Watney's Pale, as his only voluntary excursion abroad, the sort of man who'd try to travel from Islington to Istanbul and back on an undiluted diet of fish'n'chips.

'Can I buy you a pot of tea?' Carter said, 'and then, if you like, we can have a walk round the deck together.'

'Good idea,' Sam Little said. He turned to look where Olga was sitting, 'And it'll keep that queer away from you. Incidentally, you might like to ask him if they have any rice pudding. I love a bit of rice pudding.'

Seamus O'Brien telephoned to Hamburg as soon as he arrived in his own, safe, office. He missed the sailing of the *Prinz*

Hamlet by ten minutes though his observer on the docks, Gorgeous George, assured him the truck had gone on board with no sign of disturbance, and the vessel had sailed on time with no noticeable police activity in or around the dock area.

Seamus waited half an hour until the *Prinz Hamlet* would have left the main harbour and be peacefully sailing up the Elbe, then called the ship on direct ship-to-shore radio telephone. It took only ten minutes to connect him. 'Could you locate the passenger in Cabin 26? I'd like to talk to him on this number as soon as possible.'

It took only five minutes to contact the passenger in Cabin 26 over the tannoy, and another five minutes to connect the ship with the number Seamus had given. 26 sat in a glass walled booth which overlooked the radio room and waited until the radio operator had made the connection and taken off his headphones.

'Okay. What's the matter, Seamus?'

'I've just been given a hard time by AUNTIE and UNCLE. I wondered if it could be something your end?'

For AUNTIE, 26 read IMMIGRATION, for UNCLE, CUSTOMS.

'No, nothing here. The Inventory is safely locked up. I checked.'

'You still have EMMA with you?' EMMA = RADIO.

'Yes, of course. And she passes all her tests.'

'Good. I suppose the problem with Auntie and Uncle must be a coincidence. Keep watching. G'bye.'

'Goodbye.'

Walter Sievertson was descended from a long line of Hamburg seafaring men. In the dim past the family had been von Sievertson, but the *von* had been dropped many years ago. Walter had commanded seagoing vessels of most types before settling, in the days before his retirement, into the comfortable rut of taxi-ing a ferry boat from Hamburg to Harwich and back.

Compared with the heavy cargo vessels and luxurious passenger liners he had formerly commanded, the *Prinz Hamlet* was an undemanding, even cushy assignment, though in winter it could still tax his seamanship to the full. It was not for nothing that the North Sea was also known as the Mordsee, the sea of death. At fifty-nine, with short cropped snowy white hair and round pink cheeks, wearing the impeccable uniforms which were specially tailored for him in England, he looked every inch a benign benevolent wise old sea captain experienced in the ways of the world and the vagaries of the ocean, the constant demands of time and tide, the inevitable folly and mischief of those foolish people who chose to risk their lives and their health on that most untrustworthy of all nature's substances, dry land. He was eating an early Abendbrot in his cabin behind the bridge, washing it down with a half a litre of Niersteiner, the only liquid other than the sea in which he would put his trust, when the purser, disobeying explicit instructions, tapped on the door and came in.

'I'm sorry to disturb you at your Abendbrot, skipper,' he said, 'but there is a lady here I think you ought to see.'

'I'll come to your office after supper,' the captain said, pausing in his delicate negotiation of a piece of Pumpernickel covered generously with his favourite paté de fois de Strasbourg.

'I'm really sorry, skipper, really sorry, but I think you should see this lady privately.'

Captain Walter Sievertson resignedly put down the pumpernickel; it was not something to be consumed hastily between conversations.

'I see you are determined to ruin my digestion,' he said. 'As an old man, that and a love of privacy are the only passions left open to me. Bring in your lady and I will resume my supper after she and you have both gone.' He took the snowy best white Irish linen napkin the size of a tablecloth off his knee, folded it reverentially as was appropriate for an altar cloth and placed it beside his plate. He left the table and seated himself behind the desk which occupied a corner of the cabin. The purser went out and returned a few moments later with a little old lady dressed completely in black, her face hidden by a half veil. The captain rose, courteously concealing his feelings, and beckoned for the lady to occupy the chair which faced him across his desk. His look at the purser dismissed him. When the purser had gone the 'old lady' took off her veil and her hat, shook out her long blonde hair and revealed the features of a young woman. The captain had seated himself and was too old a hand to show any surprise. The lady reached into her handbag; the captain braced his hands against his desk, thoughts of piracy on the high sea, nowadays called hijacking, flooding his mind. He relaxed when the lady produced a document and a letter. He read the letter swiftly. It told him that the young lady opposite him, unlikely though it may seem in view of her age, was a senior police officer at present engaged on an investigation of the utmost delicacy and that his co-operation would be greatly esteemed. If confirmation were required it could be obtained by radio telephone reference to the Inspectorate of the Police, detective division in Hamburg, though radio silence would be appreciated.

'Before you go any further,' he said, 'please explain to me the need for radio silence.'

'The object of our investigation,' Ingrid said, 'is an Irishman of mixed Anglo-German-Irish parentage who has the intelligence and the resources to monitor any transmission made from this vessel.'

'Good. I understand that. Of course, I retain my right to make such a communication at any time I deem it necessary.'

'Of course.'

The Captain nodded, sat back in his chair, touched his fingers together, glanced despairingly at the paté de fois de Strasbourg, and waited for Ingrid to continue.

'We have reason to believe,' Ingrid said, 'that this vessel is being used as the vehicle of a smuggling racket. We believe the smugglers may be on board. We'd like to search a part of this ship, if it can be done in such a way as not to excite any curiosity. Do you think that can be done?'

'On this vessel,' he said without arrogance, 'anything I say can and will be done. But first, you have to convince me . . .'

Sam Little and Carter took another turn round the deck then went below into the bar. To the left the bar bent in an arc, dotted with red covered stools, on the right were small tables against the windows, looking out over the ocean. 'Are there waiters, or do we have to help ourselves,' Sam Little asked nervously.

'I'll get us a couple. What do you want, a beer?'

'A large whisky, if that's all right?'

'At duty free prices, anything's all right.'

Carter bought the drinks and took them to the table where Sam was sitting on one of the comfortable banquettes, his back to the ocean. Carter looked at Sam's face as he approached. It was a picture of woe. Once again he had the feeling – the wrong man doing the wrong thing, and aware of it. 'Cheer up,' he said.

Sam downed his drink in one gulp, got up without speaking and went to fetch two more. 'Take it steady,' Carter said, 'I'm not in your class when it comes to drinking.'

Sam downed the second one, too, then sat looking moodily at the empty glass.

'Is anything worrying you?' Carter said. 'Look, if you've got any sort of a problem, spill it out. What do they say, ships that pass in the night? You don't know me, I don't know you. Might be the ideal occasion to get something off your chest.'

Sam was tempted, Carter could see. 'No, no problems,' he said. 'Leastways, nothing I can't cope with.'

'Talking helps, sometimes.'

Sam got up. 'Thanks for the offer,' he said. 'But I'm afraid nobody could help me. I'm bad company tonight. What I need is bed. Thanks for the drink.'

Carter watched him walk slowly out of the bar, though he knew it wasn't the drink that impeded him, but a desire not to be alone.

Once one of the Pakistanis had used the lavatory, they all wanted to do so and Regan found himself crossing the car deck with each one, nursemaiding them in and out. The rest of the time they spent squatting in a semi-lotus positon on the floor of the truck, not talking, hardly moving. Occasionally one or other of them would start to sway gently from side to side, and then another would follow. Soon most of them would be oscillating in perfect rhythm. Regan supposed that somehow, they were able to put themselves into a state of trance, a self-imposed hypnosis that doubtless would make them oblivious to time and place. 'A damn good way of passing the time,' he thought, wishing he could do the same. As a man of action, he found sitting about in the car deck almost intolerably irksome. For the tenth time he jumped lightly down to the deck and walked along between the vans and lorries, watching the doors but stretching his legs. He had only his wristwatch to tell him the passing time, and the hands had crawled too slowly from noon to now, one o'clock at night. More than anything else he felt damned frustrated at being so near to the Tiger and being able to do nothing about him yet. But, by God, when they got to England . . .

When he arrived back at the truck he heard a new sound, that of a man moaning softly. 'If those buggers think they can start singing,' he thought, and leaped back inside the door. 'Excuse me, sir, I have to go to bathroom,' he said.

'All those bloody maize seeds . . .'

Regan gave him a hand down, rushed him across to the lavatory. The last thing he wanted was a man in the back of the truck who'd shit himself. Something about the man's blue jacket rang a bell and he realized he'd shepherded this same person across the car deck no less than four times. 'Stay in there this time,' he said, 'and get it over and done with.'

It was two o'clock when they came. The Tiger had just been to the lavatory, escorted by Regan, and they were starting to cross the car deck when they heard the noise of the handles on one of the bulkhead doors being turned. No time to get back to the truck. Regan waved to the Pakistani he'd always set to watch him when he was out of the truck. The Pakistani understood immediately, went back into the truck and pulled the door shut. Thank God they'd practised. Regan and the Tiger climbed into the van with the opened door, closed the door, and locked it behind them.

The bulkhead door opened and the Captain of the boat came in, followed by two uniformed officers. Regan cursed when he saw Carter behind them, and Ingrid. They started at one end of the line of big trucks, ignoring the cars and vans. Regan and the Tiger both watched them from the back windows of the van they were in.

'If they start checking the vans we've had it,' Regan said. 'We'll just have to give ourselves up as a pair of stowaways.'

'Not on your life,' the Tiger said, and produced a gun from his inside pocket. It was a Colt .45 and Regan remembered what he had said to Seamus O'Brien about the Mauser 7.65. The .45 was measured in inches, the 7.65 in millimetres; the bullet the Colt would fire would be almost twice as big as the Mauser bullet with many times the stopping power. His skin tingled when he remembered the 7.65 shot along it; if the gun had been a Colt, he'd have lost his hand.

What the hell could he say? 'Put that bloody thing away. Better still, hide it somewhere in the van here . . .'

The Tiger was looking at him in a curious way, a half sneer on his face. 'They told me you were Chafferty, the great big bandido from Kangaroo-Land. But you don't smell so big to me!' The safety catch was off, the gun was cocked. Regan wasn't about to argue.

While the boat's officer were inspecting the trucks with Ingrid, Carter was walking about between the vans, his eyes everywhere.

And then both Regan and the Tiger saw it. On his way across the car deck, Regan had slipped off his anorak and had thrown it carelessly across a car bonnet. 'That bloody anorak of yours, mastermind,' the Tiger hissed. 'If they see that.'

Regan could see that Carter had discovered it and was in fact working his way slowly towards it. When he came level with the back of the van, he leaned over the anorak on the car bonnet, and inconspicuously pulled it on the car deck, down the side of the van where the officers wouldn't see it. The Tiger had levelled his gun, aiming it straight between Carter's shoulder blades.

'Shall I let him have it, Chafferty?' he asked, taunting.

His mid-section ached. Coppers take a chance; that's what they're paid for. Carter had taken a chance coming down here. He'd made a mistake he bloody well ought not to have done. Regan had told him, *told* him to stay in the background. Regan's ace-in-the-hole, wasn't he?

Carter had disobeyed him yet again.

'I don't give a fuck what you do,' he whispered, 'but you'd be a bloody fool if you gave us away just yet, without any need. It looks to me as if they're checking the lorries. Time to start shooting if any of our chocolate-coloured friends has forgotten to shut his door!'

The Skipper and Ingrid had reached the side door of the Booth truck. The Skipper reached up and tried it. The handle turned. The Skipper beckoned the ships' officers forward. One of them opened the door wide and looked round inside. Regan held his breath. The Tiger levelled the gun again. Carter walked forward to join the other group.

'That's empty, Skipper,' the officer said.

The Skipper looked down a list he carried in his hand. 'The driver of that truck is in Cabin 225,' he said. 'Make a note to tell him, before he drives off, that his side door isn't fastened properly.'

'Aye, aye, Skipper.'

One by one they checked every truck; it would be impossible to know what they were looking for. Regan and the Tiger stayed where they were; the Tiger kept his gun in his hand, cocked and ready to fire. When the search was almost completed, Regan glanced at the bulkhead door through which the search party had come. It had been opened a few inches. In the gap, silhouetted against the light in the corridor outside, he could see a figure, standing still, watching. With Ingrid and Carter, down there on the car deck, who the hell could that be?

The search party didn't bother with the cars and vans. When they had finished the last lorry they left the car-deck one by one. Carter was hanging back, Regan could see, but the Skipper shooed him forward, as ever the last man to leave.

When they had gone, Regan turned to the Tiger. 'You can put that bloody thing away now,' he said. But the Tiger held the gun in his hand, down by his side, as they crossed the car deck to the truck, Regan picking up his anorak on the way. They opened the door and climbed into the back. 'Okay,' Regan said so that the Pakistanis could hear him, 'you can all come out now.' He used his key to unlock the nearest compartment and one by one they released each other. Regan went back to sit at the open door, looking out across the car deck. He was dog-tired by then, but knew he wouldn't be able to sleep. He glanced over his shoulder. The Pakistanis had readopted their semi-lotus positions and one by one were starting to weave backwards and forwards. The Tiger was standing against the back wall, the gun still in his hand.

Coppers have an instinct and, despite being dog-tired, Regan got it now. Some evasive actions you can plan. You can say, when he goes left, I'll go right. When he ducks, I'll weave. Others you can't plan, relying on the surge of adrenalin, the fast reaction, to get you through. Regan's copper's instinct told him that planning was no good. But it also told him he'd have a need of fast action, and quite soon. He hoisted his legs beneath him and into a squatting position.

It took the Tiger about five minutes to make up his mind. The first thing Regan heard was the sound of the slide of the .45 being cocked. It seemed to be a few inches behind his ear. He turned his head. He was looking straight into the barrel of the gun. And a .45 has a bloody big barrel.

'Who was he?' the Tiger asked softly.

'Who was who?'

'Don't mess me about. You know who I mean.'

Regan was prevented from replying by the Pakistani with the belly ache, who came lurching up beside the Tiger, knocking his gun arm sideways. Regan didn't move.

'Excuse me, sir, I am not wishing to disturb you but once again I must go the the lavatory.'

Regan started to uncoil himself but the gun was aiming at his head again. 'Let one of the others go,' the Tiger said quietly. With his other arm, he beckoned to the nearest Pakistani. 'You,' he said, 'take him to the lavatory.' The man he'd beckoned couldn't understand but one of the others translated for him. Regan watched the two of them cross the car deck. The Pakistani who had translated rose to his feet and spoke diffidently to Regan.

'We are all very troubled,' he said, 'to see this man who has painted his face now holding a gun in his hand. The gun will make a noise. If he makes a noise the ship men will come back and we will be found. Please convey to this man that we wish no troubles, only to come to England and our families.' He had moved a few paces forward while he had been speaking. The Tiger's left hand lashed out, a slamming sideways roundhouse that drove the air from the starved Pakistani's stomach and sent him reeling backwards, gasping.

'I shoot this bastard,' the Tiger rasped, 'and then any of you others who gets in my way, understand?' There was a quick rumble of speech and one of the Pakistanis began to keen softly in a high pitched voice.

'Thank God they were all scared to death,' Regan thought. The last thing he wanted was that lot milling about.

'Right. You haven't answered my question,' the Tiger said. 'Who is he? Why would he see your anorak and, instead of shouting about it, push it off the car bonnet to hide it?'

'You don't think I'd try something like this without an outside man, do you?' Regan asked jeering. 'What kind of an idiot do you take me for? He has a passport, he can travel openly. He looks after my back.'

'A good try. But not good enough. What was he doing on the search?'

'He's a bright lad.'

'Like I said, not good enough.'

The Highway Code gives you thirty feet of travel at thirty miles an hour and calls it 'thinking distance'. That's how far you go while you make up your mind to stick your foot on the brake pedal. It works out at less than three-quarters of a second. Regan's hand licked out like the striking head of a snake, hit the trigger guard of the Colt backwards and sideways. The backwards motion prevented the Tiger's finger closing on the trigger, the sideways motion knocked it out of his hand to skitter across the aluminium floor. Time elapsed, probably a hundredth of a second less than three-quarters, but no time to count. Other arm in stiff, aiming for the Tiger's Adam's-apple and a jab that'll knock his head off his shoulders, if it connects. But the Tiger was fast. He'd flicked sideways, half turned on the balls of his foot, elbow out, skittered Regan back against the aluminium wall. Regan bounced back hearing the Pakis spreading away, seeing the Tiger bore in, head held tucked in like a boxer. The force of Regan's backwards movement had lifted his arms high and he clenched a fist and smashed it down the Tiger's forehead, running it over the skin to the bridge of his nose. Blood gushed out of the Tiger's nose, but he'd turned sideways enough to lift his foot and kick hard sideways, chopping at Regan's shins, pushing him off balance. He felt himself falling forward and saw the Tiger's knee coming up at him and used the leverage of his feet against the bottom of the wall to launch himself forward and upwards, the flat of his forearms forward, against the length of the Tiger, who went over backwards, Regan on top of him, his forearms by now under the Tiger's throat. The Pakistanis were all jabbering but none of them came forward to interfere. The Tiger's head crashed back against the aluminium and his eyes glazed momentarily; Regan shifted his knee ready to kick upwards with it but the Tiger arched his back, slipped from beneath Regan, jumped to his feet and kicked Regan in the coccyx. Regan felt a blinding stab of pain and tried to scrabble forward. The Tiger kicked him again, driving him across the floor until

Regan's head was about a foot from the wall between the truck and the cab. The last kick seemed to travel all the way up Regan's spine and explode in his head; half conscious, he tried to turn, saw the Tiger launch himself forward in a dive that would have put both his knees into Regan's kidneys. He kicked out, swept the Tiger's feet from under him, and they both sprawled forward, jammed against the bottom of the wall with an awesome crack that could have been their skulls smashing together. Regan was winded, the Tiger was winded, and they lay side by side, looking at the wall and the hinged panel their heads had smashed in.

Regan had spent three weeks of training with the Bomb Squad.

The Tiger had blown three banks, two armoured cars, and the fat strutting President of an African Republic.

Both knew a bomb when they saw it.

'And you want me to do *nothing*?' Captain Sievertson said. 'You tell me there are smugglers on board my boat, that you have found an anorak that proves the fact, and yet, you insist I do nothing?'

Carter was out of his depth and knew it. He felt like a small boy on the carpet in the Headmaster's study. 'My Inspector will have control of the situation,' he said. 'We must leave him to carry out his intentions. After all, we're not so much concerned with this particular shipment. We want to break the organization behind it.'

'*I* am concerned with this shipment,' the Captain said. 'I have a responsibility to my company, and to myself. You didn't *see* this Inspector Regan, by any chance?'

'No, but I know he's down there, somewhere. I'm certain of that.'

The Captain looked at Olga and Ingrid. 'And you two,' he asked 'are you two, *certain*?'

Ingrid smiled ruefully. 'We know he's a resourceful police officer,' she said. 'The British seem to have a different way of going about things. In Germany we would give him overwhelming support. We'd have fifty officers on board, police boats standing by, helicopters. We'd be more thorough. I don't even think he has a revolver.'

The Captain thought for a while, as if estimating tides, wind speeds, a host of variable factors that all added up to danger or safety. 'The British Inspector is a brave man. I'm inclined to believe he knows what he is doing and to trust him. Therefore I will do as the Sergeant suggests . . .'

'And that is . . .?' Ingrid asked, seeking to cause him to spell it out.

'To do *nothing* . . . Except to get back to my bridge, if you will excuse me.'

'Radio controlled,' the Tiger said, 'a right bastard.'

'Not time controlled . . .?'

'No. Two stages. Arming, then firing.'

'Has it been armed?'

'I don't know.'

'But you could find out?'

The Tiger reared back. 'You bloody crazy? One glance should tell you that radio bomb has every-bloody-thing on it. Fail safe device. That means, if you disconnect the battery, it'll *blow*! Double detonator. That means, if you pull one of the buggers out, the other will still *blow*! Sensitized installation, that means, if you try to pull it away from where it is . . .'

'Don't tell me. It'll *blow*! So what do we do?'

The Pakistanis who had heard what they said, were now jabbering and wailing, all standing with their backs to the far wall, as if the distance could protect them. Regan needed only one glance to tell them it wouldn't. If that bomb exploded, nothing within thirty feet would still be alive. And, what's more, the hole blown in the side of the *Pinz Hamlet* would send it straight to the bottom of the North Sea. Regan got up, closed the outer door of the truck tight. 'You lot,' he said firmly. 'Sit down and shut up.'

'What about our friends in the lavatory,' one of them said.

'Let them stay there for a minute, while we bloody well think.'

He squatted down beside the Tiger. 'Let's use a bit of common sense. They can't intend to blow this while we're on board. They wouldn't risk sinking the bloody ship, now would they? Anyway, who ever works the radio switch will be on board and probably go down with it. I can't see this as a suicide mission. We're not *that* important . . .'

'I'd agree with that.'

'Secondly, there's metal all about us here. From what little I know about radio, metal acts as an insulator for radio signals. That's why you can never hear the radio when you go under a motorway bridge or in a tunnel, because of all the iron in the pre-stressed concrete.'

The Tiger was thinking deeply. 'I seem to remember one type of radio signal that cuts through anything. They use it on space ship controls. Something to do with ultra ultra frequencies . . .'

'Look, mate, we're sitting on a blasted bomb and you're talking to me about space-ships.'

The Tiger flared at him; both were feeling the strain of being so near that deadly mechanism. 'No, you look, Chafferty, or whatever your name is; it's my arse as well as yours. I take your point about whoever planted his bugger not firing it while we're on board. I think we're perfectly safe as long as we're in this hold. But the minute we leave, the minute we get out of this tin can, we'll be vulnerable. And I, for one, am not riding along the road with that thing between my legs . . .'

Regan looked at him for a long moment. 'You seem to know a helluva lot about these things,' he said finally. 'Space ships and all that; all the gimmicks. It's half past two. The boat docks just before nine o'clock. Can you make that bugger safe?'

The Tiger laughed. 'Sure,' he said, 'I can make it safe. Just give me a stethoscope, an electron gun, an oscillator, and a full set of tools.'

'There's bound to be a box of tools somewhere on this truck,' Regan said.

'I meant a surgeon's tools, you berk, not a sledgehammer and cold chisel. Anyway, if what you say is right, if they're not going to blow it while we're on board, why should I bother? Once we're through customs on the far side, nothing will keep me in this bloody death trap!'

Regan grabbed his arm. 'A dozen or more guys said something like that on the last trip. They pulled *them* out of a reservoir. Seamus O'Brien's given himself insurance for this trip.' He'd said too much, of course. The Tiger's eyes narrowed and Regan caught the glance he directed towards the Colt .45 that had skittered across the truck, estimating his chances of getting his hands on it. Regan had the advantage of being braced against the side. He dived and slid, grabbed the butt of the gun and turned round just in time to chop the round-house the Tiger was aiming at his neck.

'So you are a copper,' the Tiger said. 'I could smell you the first minute I saw you. And that man who hid your anorak, he was a copper too. All right, copper. I'll do a deal. That bastard who planted a bomb on us has got it coming anyway. I think I can defuse it. I'll need about four or five hours and it'll be tricky.' He gave a curious half smile. 'For work like that,' he said, 'you need peace of mind. Like, knowing what's going to happen to you afterwards. So, we do a deal. I fix the bomb, you forget about me when we get there.'

'You must be crazy. I could stop this boat. They could fly out a specialist bomb disposal team by helicopter. I could have that bastard safe within an hour!'

Regan was bluffing and the Tiger knew it. He was smiling and shaking his head from side to side. 'In the first place, you couldn't do all that without the man with his hand on the radio switch knowing. And secondly, if you did that, you'd wreck any chance you might have of catching Seamus O'Brien. And that's the lad you want, isn't it? Not me. I'm just one of the fish that swam into your net. You're after shark, aren't you, not small fry.'

'Get to work on the bomb,' Regan said. 'You gab too much.'

'We have a deal?'

'I don't make deals. We'll take you through customs and drop you somewhere. But I'll be making for the nearest phone.'

'I'll take a chance on that. You didn't do too well last time.'

'I wasn't the man looking for you.'

The tool kit supplied with the lorry had proved to be comprehensive; sets of all the spanners a man could want, screwdrivers, hammers, pliers, hydraulic jacks, wheel nut braces, air pumps, all of them quite useless. The Tiger extracted a knife, a pair of thin nosed pliers and an electrical screwdriver. 'You can put the rest away,' he said.

The cover came off the bomb quite easily, revealing most of the workings, even the explosive itself, evil looking bright yellow sausages that had been moulded to fit the case. Separately detonated and fused, a steel pin had been pushed through each one. The main fuse system came from each stick of explosive to a central point, through connections of small steel caps. 'Those are the self-fusing and fail-safe bits,' the Tiger explained. 'Normally, all you'd need would be to pull the explosive out. But once you take away a stick, the cap completes the electrical connection to all the others. Same with the batteries, which are hidden underneath – take one out, and the rest will blow it. It's just not possible to take them all away at once. Same with the radio tuning circuit. Knock that out, and the damn thing blows anyway.'

'So what can you do?'

'Rewire the whole thing. Make a totally separate "saddle" circuit, and then start snipping, and praying.'

'Anything I can do?'

'Yes. Keep that bloody lot quiet and out of my hair.'

Regan walked across to the Pakistanis, all of whom were squatting in the semi-lotus and waving like ears of brown barley in a gale. From each of them came a thin hollow keening sound, a rising and falling 'aieeayee' note that made his skin crawl. 'Tell them to shut up,' he said to the man who'd acted as translator. 'Tell them this man is an expert and he'll fix it all right. But only if they keep quiet and let him get on with it. Tell them, the first one who makes a noise will have to answer to me and I'll drop him over the side with an anchor round his ankles . . .'

The translator turned and gabbled rapidly in a language that seemed to Regan to have no shape other than a continuous sing-song. It worked; they were all deathly quiet.

Regan was walking back across the truck when suddenly he remembered the two men who'd gone to the lavatory. He pulled the door cautiously open and the one he'd put on watch almost fell in. 'Come quickly, Sir,' he said, 'come very quickly . . .'

Regan opened the door wide and dropped down. Before he got to the lavatory, he could hear the moans coming from inside. He pulled open the door and saw the Pakistani sitting on the seat with his trousers up, pressing his hand into his groin, obviously racked by pain. His once brown face was the most curious colour Regan had ever seen, dirty ochre yellow with distinct green tinges dark brown in the creases. He looked already dead. Regan had once seen a copper who looked like the Pakistani, though his basic colour had been sunburn. He pointed to the van. 'Get him in there,' he said, 'and lie him down.'

'What is wrong with him?' the worried guard asked, 'All day he's been trying to relieve himself. He has great trouble in the bowels, yes?'

'Bowels, hell no. That poor bugger has appendicitis.'

Regan walked quickly to the bulkhead door. What cabin number had the Captain quoted? 225? Regan opened the bulk-head door and look out. No sign of anyone. He slipped out into the corridor, closed the door behind him, then slowly made his way along to the large foyer at the end, seeing no-one. A couple of people were asleep in the armchairs in the foyer. Regan eyed the board, saw that cabin 225 would be two flights up. He went up the stairs rapidly, along a corridor without seeing anyone until he was outside 225. While he was standing there a man wearing a sailor's dungarees came along the corridor and pushed past him without taking any notice. Regan opened the cabin door and went inside. He paused, letting his eyes adjust to the almost total darkness. Four bunks in the cabin. Sam Little on the bunk facing him. He tapped the side of his face, and Sam came slowly awake, then reared up when he recognized Regan through the mists of unconsciousness. 'Get dressed quickly, and come out,' Regan hissed.

He stood there while Sam swung himself out of the bunk. One of the other sleepers stirred but didn't waken.

Sam pulled on his jacket and they left the cabin, turning right to the stern of the boat, past the cafeteria and the saloon with its sleeping passengers curling in corners hugging blankets and sleeping bags around them. The air was cold at the stern; from time to time, Regan could hear the beat of the music from the discotheque on the top deck, when the door was opened. Remembering the figures slumped at the tables of the closed cafeteria, the huddled sleepers in corners, he could understand the younger kids wanting to waste the night away in dancing, though he knew the continuous 'pop' would have driven him crazy.

'What in hell's gone wrong?' Sam Little said. 'What are you doing up here, above decks. I told you to stay where you were.'

They were standing by the rail. 'Look mate,' Regan said. 'You've got a problem. One of the Pakis has appendicitis. You'll have to bring him up here. There must be a ship's doctor on board.'

'Appendicitis. Bloody hell. You're sure?'

'Of course I'm sure. You don't think I'd come all this way . . .'

'You a doctor, or something?' Fear had made Sam Little unusually truculent. Once again Regan felt what an amateur Sam Little was – clearly the wrong man in the wrong situation, trying to cope with something far outside his experience, far too big for him to handle. They were standing at the rail on the port side by the stern; Sam turned round and smashed his hand on the rail. 'Appendicitis,' he said, 'just my bloody luck. What the bloody hell am I supposed to do now?'

Regan grabbed his arm. 'Get hold of yourself,' he said. 'We've got to bring the Paki up here, and put him somewhere they'll find him, whip him into the sickbay and look after him. You can't leave the poor bugger down there to die, and he surely will die if they don't get cracking on him.'

'But if I bring him up here, that'll blow the whole business.'

'Not necessarily. We can get him up here the same way I got up. Nobody saw me. What the hell's the matter with you?'

Sam Little had given way to the pent-up frustrations within him, the hatred of what he was doing, the fear of being found out, the anger at everything and everybody that had conspired to put him in this position. He swung out at Regan, the nearest symbol of all that anger and frustration; Regan was totally unprepared and the blow caught him in the mouth. He tasted blood and then *his* frustations gave way; within seconds they were matched, slugging each other. Regan had his back to the rail when an infuriated Sam Little, hysterical with rage and fear, slammed forward at him; Regan ducked and weaved to the side and turned, horrified, as Sam's body went straight over the rail, into the boiling white-caps of the darkened sea. Within seconds he had disappeared. Regan knew it was useless to look for him in that boiling maelstrom; there was no hope he could be found. He walked hurriedly back along the corridors to the staircase leading down. He hurried to the car-deck, opened the door, and went below. The door to the truck was still closed; the two men were in the back of the van, but the moans of one of them echoed loudly.

'Put your hand over his mouth,' Regan said. 'We're going to take him up on deck where someone will find him and bring a doctor to him.' They dragged him out of the back of the van. He was barely able to walk but they supported him through the bulkhead door and up the companionway to the upper decks. Regan's heart skipped a beat when they turned a corner and walked straight into the same sailor he had seen before; but the man smiled sympathetically.

'Seekrank?' he said. Regan didn't know what the word meant but the sailor's gesture of throwing up was all too realistic.

'Doctor?' Regan asked.

'Doktor?' He looked at the Pakistani. 'Ja, Doktor ist am besten.' He intervened between Regan and the Pakistani. 'Kabinennummer?'

Regan made a guess. 'One five five,' he said.

'Gut.' The sailor put his arm round the Pakistani and hoisted him easily, no doubt accustomed to dealing with victims of 'Seekrankheit'. By the time he had taken him through the doorway that led to the sick-bay, Regan and the other Pakistani had disappeared back down the companionway.

The Pakistani was greeted by a flood of inquiry when they reentered the back of the truck, and sat with the others, no doubt giving them a full account.

'I thought you were going to keep the bastards quiet,' the Tiger said, irritated. He wiped his face with the back of his hand wearily. Regan looked over his shoulder and saw the wires he had connected, like viscera squirming from point to point, knowing that one false connection could have blown the bomb right in the Tiger's face. 'What the hell are they jabbering about, anyway?' the Tiger asked querulously. Regan didn't blame him; the Pakis had been getting on his nerves, too.

'You know the mysterious East,' he said. 'They're holding a religious festival because one of them just managed to take a crap after being constipated all day.'

Regan beckoned over the man who'd helped him with the sick man. 'Any more noise out of them,' he said menacingly, 'and tell them I'll lock them up in the boxes, and they'll stay there until we arrive. If they live that long.'

The threat was immediately effective. Much nodding of heads, much lotus squatting, much waving backwards and forwards. But, thank God, blessed, blessed silence.

The Tiger sat back on his heels and scratched his head,

Regan looked at his red-rimmed eyes and saw the intense fatigue. 'Take a break,' he said, 'rest your eyes and your hands for five iminutes.'

The Tiger shook his head. 'I'm carrying the new circuit in my mind,' he explained. 'If I relax, I'll forget a part of it and then, bham! Kingdom Come for all of us.' He half turned his head and looked quizzically at Regan, a half smile on his face. 'How are your nerves,' he asked, 'and how steady are your hands?'

Regan knew what was coming. 'I'm no electrician,' he said quickly.

'You don't need to be.' The Tiger took up a piece of wire with red insulation, measured it against the side of the bomb, then bent the two bared ends into a rough letter U. He tried it for size again, most carefully and precisely, grunted as he bent it again.

'Where did you get the wire?' Regan asked, just for something to say to wet the inside of his mouth which suddenly had gone dry.

'There was a coil at the back of the driver's cabin. A driver always has wire, like a sailor has rope and a boy scout string.' The U-piece seemed to fit to his satisfaction. He smiled again. 'You see that brass terminal, the one between the other two?' he said, pointing with the end of the wire. There was about an eighth of an inch gap between each of the three terminals, and he was pointing to the one in the centre. 'When I tell you,' he said, 'I want you to touch one end of this wire to that terminal. Then touch the other end to this tiny silvered point. And hold them there. Do you think you can do it?'

Bloody hell! The terminal itself was small enough, about an eighth of an inch across and three sixteenths deep, but the silver spot was literally a tiny dot, no more than a sixteenth of an inch in diameter. 'Bloody hell,' he said. 'Who'd want to be an electrician? Which one do I touch first?'

'The brass one. Then the silver one. But, once you get the bridge across, don't let it slip off either until I've finished, or up the bomb goes.'

'And what are you going to be doing while I'm doing the Rutherford bit?'

'Trying my best not to jog your hand. I've got to connect the other two brass terminals together.'

'Bloody hell!'

'That's exactly where we'll be if I jog your hand.'

The First Aid man always scanned the list of passengers and isolated any with the pre-fix Doktor. One difficulty was that many people of academic rank call themselves Doktor in Germany – it was more of a courtesy title than a medical rank. A few discreet inquiries, however, and the First Aid man knew that in emergency he would have someone he could refer the seriously ill passengers to.

As soon as the Pakistani was brought into the sick bay, which already contained four sea-sickness victims and a boy who'd sprained an ankle falling down a companionway, the First Aid man realized he'd need help. 'Lie him on that bed,' he said to the sailor. 'I'll be back in five minutes.'

Dr Horst Buchmann was a gynaecologist, with a fashionable practice in Blankenese. He was travelling to England to inspect a small nursing home he was thinking of investing in; it would be a lucrative place to which to send some of his patients with 'inconvenient' pregnancies. With the pound at an all-time low, it would be a first class investment especially since he could quote all the fees in deutschmarks. He had agreed reluctantly to the First Aid man's request that he hold himself ready in case of serious emergency; had finally agreed only since he realized it would be a good thing if the Line owed him a favour. He was contemplating the value at which he'd assess his services especially being called out in the middle of the night when he walked into the first aid room, and saw at once the condition of his patient, recognizing there was not a second to lose. In that moment all the crap about fees and investments, about fashionable practices in Blankenese and Surrey, England, fell away from him. It had been a long time, hadn't it, since he'd needed to be a real doctor. And what confronted him now was the real thing. Quickly he stripped the Pakistani, felt in the man's groin and had his worst suspicions confirmed. An envelope had been taped crudely to the man's chest. It was addressed to 'The Captain', the writing obviously English. He gave it to the First Aid orderly. 'See that gets delivered right away,' he said, 'but don't take it yourself. We have work to do. What's your name – your first name?'

'Josef.'

'Right. I'll call you Joe. You ever seen an operation, Joe? A crude butcher's job? Because, believe me, that's all we have time for.'

The Captain opened the letter. Inside was one sheet of paper, hastily scribbled in English and headed FOR DET SERG CARTER ON BOARD. The Captain folded the note again and sent for the Englishman. Innately courteous, he accepted that the letter was not addressed to him. When Carter arrived, he handed it over. Carter read it, then read it again, out loud. LOOK AFTER THE PAKI. NO MORE SEARCHES, BONEHEAD. SEE YOU BY SANDBOX AS ARRANGED.

'Bonehead?' the Captain said. 'That's a very graphic phrase. I haven't met it before. Does he mean me, or you?'

Carter coloured. 'My Inspector has a funny sense of humour,' he said.

The Captain nodded. 'Even though I've never had the privilege of meeting him,' he said, 'I'm beginning to like him.'

Sweat on his brow, sweat on his hands. The cold animal stink of men in fear. Left hand on the wire on the brass terminal. Right hand, bloody thing trying to quiver, on the wire touching the tiny dot of solder. Nowhere to rest his hands or his arms to give him steadiness. Hands held out with the Tiger's hands between them as he worked the other two terminals, trying to poke a wire where a wire didn't want to go.

'Get in there, you bastard,' the Tiger muttered. Two wires already went into the terminal, coming out from beneath the aluminium plate. The terminal hole left precious little space to introduce a third wire, where no third wire was intended.

Regan's eyes ached from staring at that silver dot he was touching with the wire end and his shoulders felt an intolerable strain in them. Sweat ran down into his eyes and suddenly he could see two dots, two wires, and both seemed to waver. 'Bloody hell,' he said, 'I've got to get one of the Abduls to wipe the sweat off my face.'

'Don't for Christ's sake let that wire end go,' the Tiger said in panic. 'Not now, when I've made half the connection.'

'I can't see properly.'

The Tiger reached into his pocket, drew out an almost clean handkerchief. 'Keep your hands still,' he warned, and used the handkerchief to wipe Regan's forehead. Regan blinked his eyes rapidly to clear them of the salt solution of his sweat. 'That's better,' he said. 'At least I can only see one of the buggers now.'

As if to compensate, the wire slipped into the terminal the first try, and the Tiger was able to tighten the grub-screw that held it in position. He rocked back on his heels, flexing the muscles of his arm, and turned to look at Regan.

'Right, copper, where've you put my gun,' he said.

Regan started to sweat again. 'Is this bloody thing fixed?' he asked, but the Tiger just smiled at him. 'You don't know, copper, do you?' he said. 'You daren't let go. If it isn't fixed that's you gone. Now, where's the gun?'

'In the inside pocket of my anorak,' Regan said.

The Tiger reached over; Regan whipped the wire off the two terminals and wound it quickly round the Tiger's throat, twisting it into a loop, tight, but not tight enough to choke him. 'I'm too fucking tired to try games with,' he said. 'That sort of game, anyway.' He got carefully to his feet, then brought the Tiger upright, standing in front of him. Regan turned his body to the side to avoid a chop from the Tiger's hands. 'Into one of the boxes,' he said, grimly. He beckoned to one of the Pakistanis who opened the box lid. The fight seemed to have gone out of the Tiger, no doubt reaction against the defusing of the bomb. Regan took the wire from round his neck.

'We had a deal,' the Tiger said.

Regan slammed him in the kidneys. 'We had a deal, you bastard. Right up to the moment you pulled one from the bottom of the pack. Now it's a reshuffle, using my cards.' He slammed the lid home, turned the four clips with his tee-shaped key.

'If he makes a noise by kicking,' the Pakistani anxiously said.

'Have you ever tried to kick in rubber-soled brothel-creepers . . .?'

Number 26 stood by the partly opened door which led from the upper air shaft to the car deck, a vantage point above the tops of the trucks, the vans and the cars. The radio was silent; the microphone hidden behind the plate of the bomb no longer picking up the soft voices of the Tiger and Regan as they worked and then fought. No. 26 pressed the button; the light glowed; the bomb was 'all systems go' and could be armed and fired at any time.

The *Prinz Hamlet* docked dead on time. Carter was the first to leave the boat, leaping over the ramp as it hit the pier head. Fifteen minutes later Regan behind the wheel of the Saviem, drove along the ramp and on to the pier-side. Joe Staines was waiting for him brandishing a folder of papers. Regan reached inside the pocket of the door and found a similar wallet. He wound down the window and held it out. Joe Staines stopped when he saw him.

'I thought Sam Little had this truck?' he said.

'He did, but he was taken ill in Hamburg. The Company sent me a cable, asked me to bring it back.'

'They might have told me,' Joe grumbled. 'I've cleared Sam Little. You'll have to clear yourself with your own passport.

You've drawn Phillip Storm as Customs Officer. That's good; he's usually very quick.'

'Did you ask for him?'

'Ask for him? Not on your life. You don't ask for a particular Customs Officer here at Harwich; that's the fastest way I know to get turned over. He volunteered – probably because you had an "empty" manifest. You haven't got anything on board, have you?'

'Nothing.'

'Good. Well, I needn't hang about then, need I? I have a couple of trucks going back on the *Prinz Hamlet.* I'll need to look lively. One of 'em's got bonded stuff from the Airport. See you again, sometime, if you start regular with Booths. You could do a lot worse. They're a good company. Well, at least, they've been all right by me.'

Regan waved him goodbye, his eyes scanning the Customs shed ahead. A tall fat man came out and beckoned Regan forward, indicating he should drive into the last bay. Regan parked, pulled on the brake and climbed out. 'I'd better look inside,' the man said, 'just to make it seem right.'

No-one could hear him in the vast shed space. 'I hear your name is Phillip Storm,' Regan said, being chatty, but Storm looked quickly at him. 'Fewer the names that are handed about, the better,' he said.

Regan opened the door of the back of the truck. There was nothing to be seen. And no sound. 'Clean as a whistle, as usual, eh?'

Regan could have thrown up at the sickening complicity of this man Storm, the familiar eye-winks, the nods, the smirks. But he was too physically and mentally tired to react in the way he normally would. 'Yeah,' he said, 'as usual.'

Now the smirks had given way to a more fixed smile. 'I haven't seen you on this run before,' Storm said, 'though there is something familiar about your face. You done the run before?'

'No, this is my first time . . .'

'I could have sworn I'd seen you, somewhere.'

'On the tele, maybe. I won the Miss World contest last year. Now I'm tired. Can I get going?'

'Get going? Just like that? Don't you have anything for me?'

Regan handed him the wallet of papers he'd shown to Joe Staines. Storm opened them, riffled through them. 'Not that, you dummy,' he hissed. 'The envelope. What kind of a game are you playing?'

'Ah, the envelope. I wondered who that was for.' Regan reached up inside the dashboard of the cab, found again the envelope that had been taped there, and handed it over. The Storm kept his body between the envelope and anyone who might be watching; he opened the flap, saw the ten-pound notes and riffled through them. Regan could have told him there were ten, and was grateful again to Ingrid for supplying the forged notes from the Office of Confiscated Property of the Kriminalamt in Hamburg.

He climbed into the truck and drove to the entrance of the Customs Shed where a policeman stopped him and examined the initials the Customs Officer had crayonned on his side door. Regan leaned out of the cab and whispered. The Constable was alert; he made no overt reaction to what Regan was saying.

'Don't look up or anything. Go on examining that signature. I'm a police officer, Flying Squad. Another officer will be coming to see you in a couple of minutes. His name is Detective Sergeant Carter. Tell him Phillip Storm . . .'

The Constable nearly gave himself away, hearing a familiar name.

'Tell him, counterfeit money and that I said you're to make the arrest. That'll do you a bit of good, eh, lad?'

'Thank you very much. But, if you're pulling my leg, don't ever try to drive a truck through Harwich again, right?'

Regan drove the Saviem along the road out of Harwich, through thick mid-morning traffic. A number of cars with foreign number plates, no doubt anxious to get to Oxford Street before all the sweaters were sold, kept leap-frogging the slower line of trucks, cutting in between them often at the last minute since their drivers were on the left with restricted vision on the British roads. Regan cursed as he kept pumping the brake to avoid running into the backs of them. Inevitably, one didn't make it, disappeared off the left side of the road almost under the wheels of a ten ton CAV, through the hedge and up a tree. When Regan looked in his rear-view mirror, he saw flames begin to lick out of the engine, the holiday makers still trapped inside. He didn't stop.

Lil's transport café was the first big one on the left. He parked the Saviem behind the café, out of sight of the road, went inside, and ordered a plate of sausage, egg, chips, fried bread, with a drivers' pot of tea.

The black Jaguar that had been following him for the last two miles had pulled into the car park at the front of the café, facing out. Two men inside. The driver wearing sunglasses, a thick tweed sports cat; his mate wore a flat cap, and an anorak with a dayglow red stripe down it. Regan chose a table near the window, far from the table at which other transport men sat in a sort-of club. The two men from the Jaguar came into the café. One stood guard near the door, reading the titles on the juke box, while the other went to the counter for two cups of coffee. Then both came across to the table and sat down.

'Hello, Chafferty,' the driver said. 'What the hell are you doing with that truck. Where's Sam Little?'

Regan shrugged his shoulders. 'You tell me,' he said. 'When the time came for the truck to leave, there was no sign of him! Somebody had to bring the bloody thing away. The last thing we wanted was to be stranded in the hold of that boat, waiting for the crew to call the cops to find out why we hand't gone. So I got into the cab and drove it off.'

'And gave the agent a story about Sam Little being taken sick in Hamburg and the company sending you a wire to take his place. You think quick, Chafferty. Seamus thinks that maybe you think too quick. Like with the deutschmarks! That was a cute trick, wasn't it?'

'I'm very cute. Like Shirley Temple. Look, you berk,' Regan

said, losing his temper and reaching across the table for the driver's lapels. The driver sat there without moving; his co-driver opened his hand which contained a knife; the four-inch blade, sharpened both sides, flicked out.

'My names Harry,' the driver said, 'and this is Tom. The best shiv in the business, just in case you were interested. He can peel an orange complete in one flick, without it ever leaving his hand. That's his party trick. So, take your hands off me, eh?'

Regan played his role well; it would have been child's play to take the knife off 'the best shiv in the business', to turn his hand back and make all-bran out of Harry's jugular vein. But this was the Command Performance, and instead of an Oscar, he wanted Seamus O'Brien's head on a plate. 'Now, what were you going to tell me?' Harry asked.

'I paid ten thousand deutschmarks for this trip, and cut Seamus O'Fucking-Brien into a deal. So far, the trip's been a monumental cock-up! With me winding up behind the wheel of the bus. I'm getting pissed off. Now, let's get out of here. Give me a map or tell me where to go, and I'll deliver the truck and kiss my arse to all of you. Because, for my money, you're a bunch of bloody amateurs the like of which I've never seen before.'

Tom stabbed downwards with the knife. It stuck into the wooden table top, between Regan's fingers. 'That could have been the back of your hand, sweetie,' he said. 'Button your lip when you're talking to Harry. He doesn't like bad language.'

Before he could utter another word, Regan had jerked the knife out of the table and had smashed the butt end against Tom's adam's apple.

'And that could have been the fucking point, sweetie,' he said, 'And Harry can stick what he likes and doesn't like right up his you-know-where. Now get on that radio telephone in the Jag, and tell Seamus I'll deliver his load anywhere he likes, or I'll dump it right here. Tell him to make up his mind; I don't give a damn which!'

They both got up and went towards the door. 'You forgot

this,' Regan said and threw the knife in a graceful arc. It stuck in the wooden door surround next to Tom's arm. He cursed and they went out. Regan followed them and stood beside the driver's side of the car; Harry tolled the window up while they asked for the number, rolled it down again when the connection had been made. 'We've made contact,' he said, 'and the client wants to bring the truck all the way through.'

He listened for a while, turned and smiled at Regan. 'It'll still cost you the ten,' he said.

'I don't care about that. Where do I take it to?'

'Bletchley. Know where it is?'

'Yes.'

'Main north road into Bletchley. There's a cement and gravel pit on the right-hand side of the road. Drive in there and park behind the heap of gravel. Understand?'

Regan nodded, turned on his heel and walked round the café to the Saviem. A piece of string was hanging over the driving wheel, with nine knots in it. He drove the Saviem out of the car park, following the Jaguar on to the main road westwards. After a mile, the Jag pulled into the side and let the Saviem pass, pulling out again on to its tail to the evident disgust of another lorry, which flashed its lights and hooted, its horn. Regan saw Harry reach his arm out and make the V sign, and the lorry dropped back. Carter had parked the Cortina at the far end of a lay-by. The sand-box was in the centre of the hundred foot tarmac strip, with overflowing waste bins each side. Regan halted the Saviem between the sand-box and the Cortina, pulled on the hand brake, switched off, and climbed down. The Jaguar had stopped at the beginning of the tarmac, and Tom, the 'best shiv in the business', scrambled out and into the small wood behind the lay-by. Regan stood by the sand-box, waiting. Harry climbed out of the Jag and walked slowly towards him, his right hand in his pocket.

'What do you think this is, a remake of High Noon?' Regan said as he flipped open the lid of the sand-box. He dug in the sand with his hand, located the plastic bag and drew it out. He was going to put his hand into it when Harry snatched it away, opened it, and took out the torn notes. Regan didn't try to stop him as Harry backed away, conscious that Tom was somewhere in the woods behind him. Carter was there, too, with strict instructions to lie doggo. Maybe this time, he'd do what he'd been told. Regan stood still; he saw Harry pick up the telephone and waited. Then Harry put down the telephone, flashed his lights and blew his horn. Tom reappeared out of the woods and climbed into the Jaguar, which burned rubber on its pull-away, streaking back east down the road.

Regan climbed into the Saviem, and drove westwards, towards the cut off that would lead him to Bletchley.

Number 26 watched him go, put away the telescope, climbed into the Mercedes, and set off, following about a half a mile behind the Saviem, safe from observation.

The Intensive Care Unit of the Marine Mission Hospital had been generously endowed by rich ship-owners in its past; now it was part of the larger National Health Services but still well-equipped for its size. They were used to receiving emergencies from ships, often too late to do anything constructive. The Pakistani had been brought from the *Prinz Hamlet* in an ambulance with its sirens going full blast, its lights all flashing. Harwich residents moved out of the way of the accustomed sight; the tourists took longer to register.

Dr Horst Buchmann rode in the ambulance, his finger constantly on the Pakistani's pulse, his stethoscope ready to check heart beat. The operation had been a near thing; they'd reached the appendix just after it had burst but, with luck, they could avoid the killer, peritonitis, always a complication following a burst, when all the poison the appendix is designed to contain leaks into the system.

The Intensive Care team swung into immediate action; the Pakistani was put on to oxygen and the life support systems were plugged in to assist respiration after the shock of the shipboard operation. The Medical Officer in charge of the Intensive Care Unit listened to Dr Buchmann gravely, then examined the wound. 'You did a very good job, Doctor, considering the working conditions,' he said. Dr Buchmann smiled in tired pleasure. 'It's been a long time since I've done any real surgery,' he said. Now that he'd handed over his patient, he felt lost, lacking any sense of direction. The hospital provided a car, and he was driven back to the *Prinz Hamlet*.

The Pakistani lived for thirty minutes, during which, it was later assessed, at least fifteen people, doctors, sisters, nurses and technicians all completely gowned and wearing masks, entered and left the Intensive Care Unit.

Thirty minutes after he arrived, and without regaining consciousness, the Pakistani died.

It was that dull half hour before dusk when Regan pulled into the sand and gravel pits on the outskirts of Bletchley. He drove the Saviem along the pitted roadway, past the parked gravel lorries, the two cement mixing towers, the gravel grading hopper, the rotating crusher. About half a mile down the track ahead, through two high wire-meshed steel gates, he could see a complex of huts, from the top of one of which extended a sophisticated radio antenna system, justified, no doubt, to the authorites by the radios in the cabs of the parked gravel lorries. He brought the Saviem to a halt behind a sixty-foot heap of mixed sand and gravel from which the premix concrete lorries would be loaded. He stepped down from the cab and stretched his arms and legs, the total picture of relaxation. His tiredness was forgotten; though he didn't look it, he was completely alert, every nerve-end in his body tingling for the action he knew would soon come.

Seamus didn't disappoint him; he had an Irishman's love of the dramatic, a sense of theatre, a feeling for occasion. Before he could know what was happening, Regan found himself surrounded by minibuses which seemed to have materialized from nowhere. Each had its headlights full on. Each halted with a squeal of brakes a mere six feet from Regan. The Saviem behind him, the mini-buses in front. Regan was trapped. The men in the mini-buses sat silent, looking through the windscreens over the curtain of lights. Their engines were stopped as quickly as they had been started and revved up. An eerie silence fell over the gravel pits. A duck cawked on the lake the gravel excavations had made. Traffic rumbled along the main road outside.

And then Regan heard the chuckle of Seamus O'Brien's voice. 'Nice to see you again, Mr Chafferty.' He whirled round and saw Seamus standing at the back of the Saviem. 'And thank you for taking the trouble to deliver my clients to me . . . Safe and sound, I trust?'

'See for yourself . . .'

'Oh, I shall, dear man, that I shall!'

Seamus opened the side of the truck and from it spilled a small sea of brown faces, leaping down to the ground, the beloved dreamed-of ground of England. They were all smiling like schoolboys or mischievous monkeys, clutching their arms around each other, hugging each other and themselves.

'We've no time to waste, boys,' Seamus said. He counted the heads, turned to Regan. 'You appear to have lost one, Mr Chafferty. Not still in the truck, is he?'

'My guess is he's in hospital in Harwich by now. He had an appendicitis. I had him taken care of by the ship's doctor . . .'

'Did you now? Mr Chafferty, you're a man of infinite resources. A true professional. 'Tis a pleasure to do business with you. And don't worry about him talking to the authorities, don't you worry your little head about that. They placed him in the Intensive Care Unit. The poor divil. What a tragedy. He was doing so well, too, until someone inadvertently exchanged the oxygen bottle for nitrogen!'

Regan shrugged his shoulders. 'Am I my brother's keeper?' he said. Inwardly he seethed. That was one he hadn't thought of. He'd known they'd take the Paki off and get him into a hospital as soon as possible, but thought that O'Brien's people at Harwich would be too interested in what was happening to the Saviem to bother about the ambulance leaving the dockside. One more nail in O'Brien's coffin, one more peg on which to hang the hatred he felt for him, trafficking in this most inhuman racket of them all. He looked around the Pakistanis; wondering what the hell was going to happen to them. Would Immigration listen to his special pleading? He was going to give them the Tiger, break up a ring that must have brought tens of thousands of such people into the country. But would the frost faces of Immigration melt, would they, could they, condone the crime these men were committing by being here, illegally?

'That's a very sensible attitude for you to take,' Seamus said. 'Now, let's not keep our brothers longer out of the arms of their loved ones than is strictly necessary. Which one of them speaks English?'

Regan pointed to the man who'd translated for him. The man stepped forward and O'Brien produced a list, like a travel courier assigning people to hotels. 'These are the names,' he said. 'To tell the truth, I can't make head nor tale of them. You'll see I've put numbers beside each name and if you look at the mini-buses, you'll see they've all got numbers on the windscreens. Number One is for Brixton, Number Two for Solihull, got it? Get your men in there as fast as you can, and they can leave the yard at five minute intervals.'

'Very good, sir,' the Pakistani said. 'Rely on me, sir. I was sweeper at Rawalpindi Railways Station, understanding all matters of transportation. With me, everything go tigatebu!'

'Dear man,' Seamus said, 'Tigatebu, that's how we want it.'

It took only minutes for the Pakistanis to divide and subdivide the group throughout the mini-bus transports. As soon as they were all on board, Seamus waved the first one away. He backed off slowly, went up the track without lights on, then sped left, south into the gathering dusk. The five minutes was changed to two, and soon the gravel yard was empty. Except for Seamus O'Brien, the Saviem truck, Jack Regan, and the Mauser in Seamus O'Brien's hand.

'Now, Mr Chafferty, let's find out who you *really* are. Get in the truck, carefully, and drive me down the road a bit, to that hut. And I needn't say again that if I have to kill you, I don't have the slightest objection, do I?'

As Regan went round the truck to the driver's side, he quickly transferred the Tiger's Colt .45 from his inside pocket to the inside of the top of his socks. The end of the muzzle went down his shoes uncomfortably, but it had a better chance there of being missed.

Seamus didn't climb into the cab; he stood on the running board step, holding the door open, the Mauser levelled across the seat top. 'Take it steady, Chafferty, won't you,' he said. 'I'd hate for this thing to go off on its own, especially pointed at your throat this way.'

Regan was reminded of a film he'd seen on the television, years ago before he joined the Sweeney, Yves Montand at the wheel of a lorry full of explosives – Wages of Fear, was it called? – over pitted roads. He guided the Saviem more carefully than it had ever been driven before, through the gates which were opened for him by dour-looking men carrying shotguns, past the edge of the lake of the gravel pit, ignoring the raucous cries of the moorhens, the odd looking ducks, flying about its surface. No time for the Peter Scott bit. No time for anything but that truck and the deep ruts, that Mauser pointing at this throat.

He stopped the Saviem outside the open door of one of the huts.

'A humble place,' Seamus O'Brien said, 'but mine own. Now get down, very carefully. Come round the front of the cab. I needn't tell you what a shotgun can do at close range, need I? No, I guess I needn't.'

Regan climbed out, walked round the front of the truck and into the hut where Seamus was already waiting. His eye quickly took in the scene; the schedules on the wall indicated that Seamus really did run a sand, gravel and premix concrete business. But the bank of radios mounted against the wall gave a clue to his real intention.

'We have a nice little business here,' Seamus said as he waved Regan to a chair, 'too nice to let somebody like you mess it up. Now tell me what you did with your other passenger?'

Regan was calculating. 'Say twenty Pakistanis a week. My guess is that they don't have to pledge ten thousand deutschmarks – five would be more like it. So much down, and the rest taken out of the social security once they get here. However you cut it up, means a hundred thousand deutschmarks a week, that's thirty thousand pounds in these devalued days. Not bad. Say the actual organization, lads like Harry, your people in Germany, cost you ten thousand a week, that still leaves you a profit of twenty thousand a week, a million a year. Come to think of it, you probably sell these Pakis to a broker. He gives you five thousand deutschmarks cash for them, buys their earning power, and probably recovers twice as much from the poor bastards who know no better. It's the bloody slave traffic, all over again!'

Seamus was looking admiringly at him. 'You've got it all worked out, that's for sure. You've got a few of your figures wrong but I don't mind correcting them for you. The take is five times what you say. I've agencies working for me in all the cities of both India and Pakistan. So, the expenses are larger. I reckon we show only a fifty per cent net. Pity, but then, we don't pay taxes, you see.'

'Two and a half million a year. That's big money.'

'It certainly is.' Seamus leaned forward on his desk, a sweet smile on his face. 'And do you know where most of it goes? I'm not a man for the creature comforts. I give myself a bit of luxury sometimes in Hamburg, but this is my spiritual home, if you'll excuse the expression. Here, in my drab little office, with my radios working quietly. Earning money that I can spend buying weapons and ammunition for the poor lads back home. To kill lads like you with. And I'll tell you this much; I'm Irish. I don't give a hoot whether its the Catholics or the Protestants. I supply them all. Because all any decent Irishman wants to do, is kill you Englishmen. To kill the lot of you that ever set foot in Ireland. And if, while we're doing it, we can foul up your country with these Pakis, crowding them into your cities, your social security services, then that's a blow for the future. They all breed like rabbits, you know. That's a laugh. All your frigid English ladies saying, let's restrict it to two and a half kids, while this lot are at it night and day. And the only man who has sense enough to see what's happening is working as a Member of Parliament from that slave state, Northern Ireland. 'Tis a beautiful situation, Mr Chafferty-whatever-your-name, a most beautiful situation. And you must have been crazy to think you could come into it and break it apart. Though I will say this for you, you're a professional, like myself, a professional. So you won't mind having to pay the price, now will you?'

'You don't know what's happened to Sam Little and the Tiger, yet.'

'There, my friend. I knew you'd give yourself away if I waited long enough. How the devil did you know he was the Tiger? And as for not knowing where he is, I'm afraid you underestimate me. He's locked away behind one of the panels at the back of that truck. Sam Little had the misfortune to meet a professional. Very clever the way you got him over the side. Very resourceful; but then, I've admired you as a resourceful man since the first time we met outside Karstadt. Don't you worry about the Tiger. That trip was the last with Mr Booth's trucks, unfortunately we're going to have to work out a new method. I'm afraid that truck is going to have a nasty accident. With the Tiger still locked away safe inside it. And, by the way, you at the wheel!'

The time had come for plain speaking. 'You can stop calling me Chafferty,' Regan said. 'My name is Jack Regan. Inspector Jack Regan of the Flying Squad. I came on the case when fourteen bodies were found dead in the reservoir, working with the Bletchley Police. I've got enough on you to send you down for life, either here or in Hamburg. I was working with the Police over there . . .'

'Ah, yes, my dear Ingrid. Such a nice girl, I've always thought, and so misplaced in her job, don't you agree?'

'Okay, wise guy, so you can make intelligent guesses. Can you guess that Hamburg at this moment, is busy turning over all your operations?'

Seamus looked exasperated. 'I thought you were more of a professional than that, Regan,' he said. 'Do you think I would organize a business like this without taking a few elementary precautions? I *know* the Hamburg police are – as you so quaintly put it – turning over all my businesses. I *planned* it that way. It takes care of all my redundancy problems if the police pick them all up for me. Why do you think I use my own name all the time, Regan? Because I don't care. All the men in Hamburg will be saying – oh, I'm not the leader. You must look for a Mr Seamus O'Brien. They can look all they want, but they won't find me. Next time, I'll probably set up shop, if I need to, in Cuxhaven, or Bremerhaven. Or work out of Holland, Belgium or France. Flexibility, *Mr* Regan, is the secret of success in criminal life. You know my name. By now you've seen whatever dossiers the Flying Squad and the Special Branch may have on me. But you haven't got *me*, Regan, locked up in a cell. And you never will have. This Mauser will tell you why. You see, nobody wants to die, do they? And you would die before ever they got me near a cell. Now, let's go outside and put an end to this charade. All you have left right now, Regan, is your dignity. Try to keep it, if you can.'

They went out into the yard together. Seamus looked around him, surprised. 'Harry?' he said out loud, 'Tom?'

There were no replies.

'Fred? Sam, Albert?'

A bird honked across the water of the gravel pit, flying low.

The dull evening had given way to an exhibition sunset, reds and yellows streaking across the horizon like a painter gone mad or a pop-art poster. Each tree on the opposite bank of the pit was outlined with harsh clarity in that last daylight fling.

Regan breathed in deeply. 'Nice evening, Seamus?' he said: then he called out. 'Right-o, lads. Let's have a few names.

Starting clockwise from the truck.' He held out his arm in a deliberately dramatic gesture, his eyes boring into Seamus's. The slow phlegmatic voices came out of the sunset, a Gilbert and Sullivan chorus line. 'Jones', 'Richardson', 'Williams'. There was even a 'Docherty', and an 'O'Malley'. Regan counted nine names altogether, the same number as the knots on the string looped over the steering wheel when he came out of Lil's café. Carter had been busy; he'd cleared out the Pakis into the lavatory, silently installed the Flying Squad men, and brought the Pakis back, none the wiser; while Regan kept Harry and Tom busy with his knife act. The nine Flying Squad men had travelled in the spaces inside the Saviem, a true Trojan Horse.

Seamus was quick; he darted behind Regan, held his gun with the barrel an inch from his back, level with his heart.

'Very clever, Regan,' he said. 'And very dramatic. You should be directing them at the Abbey. Now tell them all to come out where I can see them.'

Regan did as Seamus told him, and the men appeared from their various hiding places. Two of them, Docherty and O'Malley, were carrying regulation Servicemen's Lee Enfield .303. rifles. The accurate one, with the high back-sight. Superintendent Maynon nearly had a fit when Carter asked him to authorize the application for two police marksmen, on the grounds that all O'Brien's men were armed, but the Commander listened to the application and gave his authorization immediately. The marksmen knew they must operate under strict conditions, and, above all, could not fire unless ordered to do so by the 'Scene of the Incident' officer. Nobody had told them, however, what to do when the 'Scene of the Incident' officer had a Mauser stuck near his heart. They carried the rifles by their sides. Regulations also specify that a marksman must only fire a rifle by aiming it correctly – none of this Iwo Jima firing from the hip.

Regan looked round him. Where the hell could Carter have placed himself? Not that Carter would have a gun. Two possibilities. In that clump of shrubs down by the edge of the water of the gravel pit. Behind the huts, somewhere? On the ramp of the loading chute? He could be anywhere. Seamus tapped Regan's pockets and found no evidence of a weapon. 'Don't try any of that fancy karate stuff, will you?' he said into Regan's ear. 'You and me are staying close, like this. Any sign of movement out of you and I'll shoot. You see, Regan, I have one advantage over you. I believe in something. You believe in nothing. You're doing a job for which you get paid. One day, they'll give you a pension. I'm doing a job for which there's only one end. One day, I'll get killed. But I won't be the first or the last man to die for Ireland. Oh, I know you're saying I'm a fanatic. Well, boyo, just remember it's true. 'I *am* a *fanatic.* And that's what gives me the edge over you, and every other Englishman that was ever misbegotten.'

Regan grunted. 'Cut out the bloody speeches,' he said 'I'd rather you shot me than bored me to death. Which is what you're doing now.'

They walked together, too close linked for the police to do anything, towards the Saviem. They had almost reached the cab when the door of the Saviem was flung open. The Tiger stood there, holding an army Sten gun in his hands, the clip on it.

'You didn't know about these, did you copper?' he said. 'Tell him, Seamus, how Pakistanis are only part of your cargo. Tell him about all these Sten guns and all this ammunition your lads get from the British Forces in Germany. And then smuggle to Ireland to use against the British Forces there.' He pressed the trigger but Regan and Seamus alike were both half-way to the ground. The muzzle of the Mauser had caught in the back of Regan's coat. Regan rolled, looking back. The police were down, too, and neither Docherty nor O'Malley would be firing rifles for a time.

He heard the crack of the Mauser and rolled back again; now he was facing the truck and saw the spurt of blood along the Tiger's left arm, which hung useless at his side. The Tiger lifted the Sten gun one handed, pulled a burst on the trigger. The rounds shot along the gravel top towards them, picking up spurts of dust. Regan threw himself violently sideways, saw the

Mauser spin out of Seamus's hand. Regan's hand went down to his ankle for the Colt .45 but it had fallen out of his sock when he had thrown himself so violently to the ground.

He looked around quickly. The Colt was ten feet behind him. No chance to get to it. Seamus was lying flat on his back, blood oozing from his shoulder. The Tiger jumped out of the back of the Saviem, waving the Sten, and climbed into the truck. He propped the Sten over the window. Nobody moved. They heard the engine turn over and start, and then the Saviem roared away along the path.

Regan dived for the nearest rifle and got it. He turned round, threw himself down on the ground adjusted the back-sight, took careful aim at the right hand back tyre. Safety catch off? Gun cocked? He pressed the trigger and the gun went off. The round spurted dust from the path along which the Saviem was careering. He took aim again, re-sighting to two hundred yards the estimated distance of the truck. He squeezed the trigger, and the whole Saviem exploded into a million fragments, creating a shock wave that sent the gravel and sand whanging back along the road to them, slashing into Regan's face, like the buckshot of a shotgun. A column of fire and smoke rose into the air for about a hundred feet, flaring into reds and yellows, and the shattered parts of the truck whined in the air above them, whistling like banshees. The water of the surface of the gravel pit was whipped to a frothing storm; two trees by the side of the path snapped and roared through the air sideways, their branches snapping and crackling like Jumping Jacks. And then the boom came, one single ear-stunning compression of air that brought tears to Regan's eyes and rang his head like a bell, as if giant hands had been clapped simultaneously on both sides of his skull.

Seamus was the first to recover; he skittered like a crab across the gravel surface, came into a crouch with the Colt .45 in his hand, crabbed back until, once again, he was bending over Regan.

'Nothing's changed, Mr Regan,' he said, 'except that I've taken your advice and got myself a larger calibre of gun. If I'd had this in my hand pointing at that devil I wouldn't have lost all them valuable Sten guns, now would I?'

Regan shook his head, but not to agree with the Irishman, to clear some of the ringing from it. He looked at the nine men, all getting up slowly from the ground. 'How many of you were hit?' he asked. Four of them replied. He turned to Seamus. 'Come on, you silly sod,' he said in total exasperation. 'Let's get this bloody lot over and done with.'

The two of them got to their feet. 'Behind the shed,' Seamus said, his voice hoarse from the flying dust, his eyes desperate with a kind of madness that told Regan he wouldn't listen to reason.

A 4.2 litre Jag was parked behind the shed. Automatic. Radio, stereo, cigar lighter, electric windows, all mod cons.

'You drive,' Seamus said.

Regan pulled open the door. 'This is the biggest, bloodiest, waste of time I've ever heard of,' he said. 'Why the fucking hell don't you wake up to the fact. You've lost out, Seamus; now it's my turn to say – you're dead.'

'Get in and drive.'

They got in and Regan started the engine. 'Look. There are police blocks on the roads,' he said. We've already taken the Pakistanis into custody. You haven't a hope in hell of getting through, you know that.'

Seamus was grinning. 'You always underestimate me, Regan,' he said. 'Drive the car, there's a dear man!'

Regan put the control lever in drive, took off the handbrake and rolled the car forwards. When they turned the side of the hut, the nine men were waiting there. Two of them had picked up the rifles. Regan halted, used the switch to wind the window down electrically. 'Stay out of it, lads,' he said. 'Look around here and you'll find a first aid kit somewhere.'

'That's very sensible of you,' Seamus said. Regan didn't reply, turned the car down the track, drove slowly to the edge of the crater that once had been the Saviem truck. Water had already seeped into the bottom. He drove cautiously round the right-hand rim, then back on to the roadway. The two gates had been either left, or blown, open. The main road lay ahead. 'Which way,' he asked, as if he didn't give a damn. 'We have police traps either way, north or south.'

'North,' Seamus said.

The traffic was light along the road, with at least five hundred yards between vehicles. No doubt the road blocks were chopping up the steady stream, diverting any vehicles just passing through.

They'd gone half a mile when Seamus said, 'Watch out for a gate on the left of the road. About five hundred yards ahead.'

Regan cursed. The road block was at the roundabout, at least a mile away. Seamus was smiling at him. 'Professional,' Seamus said, 'and you shouldn't forget it.'

Regan could see the gate. 'Now, here's what you do,' Seamus said. 'You slow down, wait until that van behind us has gone past.'

He did as he had been told. 'Now, line yourself up on that gate, turn off your lights, and drive with your foot down, straight through it. You'll find the gate's only held up by bits of thin string and it'll flop down in front of you.'

It did; Regan doubted it had even scratched the paintwork. They were in a field with a cart track running alongside a hedge. About a half a mile along the track, the hedge suddenly turned to the right and a fold in the field was revealed, a short wide valley which contained a long low barn. One or two trees were dotted about; a couple of cows wandered in the half-light of the coming evening.

Regan accelerated when they'd turned the corner, driving into the valley. 'What's in the barn?' he asked. 'A submarine?'

Seamus chuckled. 'You'd be surprised,' he said. 'And, by the way, don't bother accelerating the car, thinking you can drive it into one of these trees. In the first place, the car has a strengthened chassis, and in the second case, I'd kill you before we ever got near.'

Regan eased off on the accelerator. 'You read my mind,' he said.

Seamus slapped his left hand on his knee; the gun didn't waver in his right hand. 'Regan, you're a trier,' he said. 'For an Englishman, you earn my respect. You're not Irish are you, by any chance?'

'As Irish as Bow Bells.'

''Tis a pity. Right, drive the car to the side of the barn and park it.' Now the gun was held against Regan's temple. 'Don't make me do it, will you,' Seamus said.

The car stopped. Regan turned the key to halt the engine, wound down the driver's window, using the electric button.

Ahead of him, he could see that the barn was, in fact, much deeper than he had supposed. Only ten feet showed above ground but a ramp lead down the far end to a further depth of about fifteen feet, giving the barn a total ceiling height of about twenty-five feet. Neither from above, nor from casual observation from the side, could the depth of the barn be seen.

'Not a submarine, you see,' Seamus said. 'A helicopter. Very useful for flying under radar screens, for picking up from vessels at sea, for running away from inquisitive policemen.'

Regan turned his head. Seamus held the gun steady, the muzzle scraping lightly across Regan's skin until it was levelled to his forehead, neatly above and between his two eyes. He didn't blink. 'Seamus,' he said. 'Wherever you go, whatever you do, I'll be looking for you. One day, I'll find you. One day, I'll stand up in a court and give evidence against you. And that's a promise.'

'I like you! I *like* you!' Seamus said, his voice expressing only delight. 'Regan, you're a man after me own heart. To think you can sit there, in the last seconds of your life, and say that to me, is truly worthy of an Irishman. You've got the nerve of the devil himself. I'll tell you what I'm going to do.' He reached out his left hand and flicked open the cupboard on the passenger side. 'Look in there,' he said, 'if you can do it without moving your head too much. You'll find a pair of handcuffs. Get 'em out, and clip yourself to the wheel.'

Regan swivelled his eyes, saw the handcuffs, brought them out, and examined them.

'German,' Seamus said. 'You'll never open *them* by banging the sides of them, the way you can with these cheap English jobs. Now put them on.'

Regan clipped one bracelet round his right wrist. Seamus took the other, passed it round the steering wheel, and clipped it round Regan's left wrist. Then he put the gun down.

'Life's been very dull for me recently,' he said, as if he were sitting in the Confessional. 'You'll brighten it up a bit. The knowledge of you, sitting in an office somewhere, biting your fingernails, wishing you could lay your hands on Seamus O'Brien. I can't think of anything that'll make me happier during the long nights ahead. I'll be a cancer that'll grow inside you, Regan. Mark my words. The name of Seamus O'Brien will bring the bile to your throat and tears to your eyes. And when, one day, in some corner of an official report, you hear they've got me at last, you'll rant and rave and curse that your hand wasn't the one that pulled the trigger. I shall think about you, Jack Regan of the Sweeney. I shall remember you, sitting here in this Jaguar when they find you and get the bolt cutters to you, and the word seeps through the force of how they had to pick up your pieces when Seamus O'Brien bested you.'

He got out of the Jaguar. 'I am even going to leave you the key,' he said, 'just to give them a good laugh when they find you.'

He walked away from the car without looking back. Regan saw him enter the barn, heard after a few minutes, the sound of an engine turning over, the large doors at the far end of the shed being opened, running sideways and folding back on oiled rollers.

He slid his hands as far towards the key as he could, stretched out his fingers. No hope of reaching it. Head sideways, legs up and over the back of the seat, head down under the wheel; wrists twisted, never mind the pain that feels as if they're breaking. Mouth against the dashboard, searching. Key against his nose, on his lip, in his mouth. Twist his head and turn it. The engine twirls. Damn. Twist again, engine turns again, fires, bend his head down and swing round past the wheel, well, that's the theory but he's moving fast and the wheel bangs against the bridge of his nose and brings tears to his eyes. Elbow sideways, straining, pulling the chain tight against his wrists to a cutting pressure but what the hell, his elbow has to, has to, *has to* reach the front of the handbrake. Bangs it, releasing it. The hand brake lever springs forward. Other elbow sideways, again the pull on his wrists, and now the helicopter appears, the movement of the vane bringing it slowly out of the shed towards the bottom of the ramp. Twist his body to get that extra fraction of an inch, and then, reach the selector lever for the automatic and slam it into low drive. The helicopter starts to move slowly on to the ramp, gathering speed, the rotating vane about two feet below the level of the side of the ramp. Footbrake on, rev the engine to the near stall point then quick release the foot brake and the car leaps forward. Twist his thumbs backwards, no good, lean forward, grasp the wheel with his chin and the sides of his forearms and wild-eyed aim the car straight for the edge of the side of the ramp. The blade swinging round just below as the edge draws near, like the blades of a mincing machine, and a last sickening thought, will the blades chop somehow through the floor of the car, but no time to worry now, smash the accelerator all the way down, aim the Jaguar with his chin. Rev like hell, head pushed backwards as far as it will go, brace with both feet, one on the accelerator one on the floor and the Jaguar took off over the edge, sailing through the air. Quick flashing thought, what a fuck-up if it flies right over the top, but the weight brings it down, down in a sickening nose forward lurch and time to see Seamus's face as the Jaguar crashes down on top of the blades, stopping them instantly, shearing them, banging tyre, flood of oil from somewhere, stink of petrol and the perspex of the cockpit being smashed with a terrible sick rending sound that includes the splintering smash and the overwhelming scream from Seamus's lips as the whole weight of the Jaguar motor drops out of the sky straight on to the top of his head. Silence. Faint crackle of oil. Don't let the car burn! Don't let the petrol hit anything and burn! Don't please let me end my life a flaming torch! The Jaguar tipped forward, creaking along its seams, slid down the shattered hulk of the helicopter. Regan's right leg was broken, or at least it felt like it. Tip down, down, then slide with a terrifying screech of metal against metal, the snap of the rotary gear of the helicopter, then the car plunging crazily, its wheels, stripped tyreless, hitting the ground first and rolling forward and then the back sliding and scratching down the side of the wreckage. A noise, an odd noise. Regan's eyes blinked. The engine of the Jaguar was still running! His foot had slipped off the accelerator pedal; he put it back on and pressed it and the Jaguar made a horrible screech but still moved forward, if you could call it 'moving', this wobbling action, which flung him from side to side as the Jaguar climbed over the last obstacle and banged forward scraping its right front wheel on the concrete ramp and wobbling from side to side as the rims ground into the roadway and the inside of the mudguards. Water was boiling out of the underside of the bonnet and there was a stink of burning oil and wires but slowly, with an infinity of groans and shudders the car made its gallant way up the ramp to the top, finally coming to rest and expiring on the grass overlooking the torn tangled squashed remains of what once had been a helicopter and its pilot.

The car door was yanked open. 'Are you going London way?' the voice of Carter said. 'Give us a lift?'

'Cheeky bugger,' Regan said, and passed out.

When Regan came round he was lying on the grass without the handcuffs. 'The key was in the glove compartment,' Carter said, 'you could have reached it with your toes . . .'

'How long have I been out?'

'Only a couple of minutes.'

'You got a car?'

'Yes.'

'Get me back to the Quarry, quick.'

When they arrived outside Seamus's office, Ingrid was standing there, with Superintendent Maynon, DCI Haskins, and

Chief Superintendent Mackenzie. She looked at Regan, long and hard. 'You know?' she said.

Regan nodded.

He looked around the site; only one place was left where a person could hide and still be in line of vision with the office; the small wood on the other side of the lake, rising slowly up the hill, but not going all the way. A radio, not my bullet, exploded that truck,' Regan said.

'I think this is mine,' Ingrid said.

'Ours.'

'If that's the way you want it.'

'Yes.'

He walked across to the constable who was holding the rifle. 'I'll take that,' he said. Haskins and Mackenzie were muttering together, but Superintendent Maynon hushed them with a gesture. He came to Regan. 'You know the rules,' he said. 'Only if you have to . . .'

'I know.'

Ingrid and he set out, side by side, walking alongside the water. They didn't speak. At the end of the lake, they turned right to follow the edge of the water round, then headed at an angle to the lake, slowly climbing the hill until they were above the small wood. They walked upright to the edge of the wood, then crouched down. It was almost dark and the trees were softened by the dull grey light, surrendering their outlines. Slowly they worked forwards, a tree at a time. Birds sang briefly then were silent. Ingrid was reminded of Ueber allen Gipfeln ist Ruh! The birds are silent in the trees. Wait awhile, soon, you too will know a peace. Would *she* know peace? This man beside her had asked her why did she continue with her job among the scum of the Reeperbahn in Hamburg. How could she tell him in a way he could comprehend that she had to stay in the Reeperbahn because of a kind of love he couldn't understand, a love that didn't exclude any feelings she might have for him, but yet was all demanding.

They advanced slowly forward into the centre of the wood. Now it was almost impossible to make out any clear shapes, the overhead branches cutting out the last of the direct light, suffusing only a faint greyness that obliterated all colours to a uniform grey green.

They stopped; the edge of the wood was fifty yards ahead of them.

'We know you are there,' Regan said, softly. 'We know you worked the radio that blew up the truck. The Tiger is dead. Seamus O'Brien is dead. You can come out now.'

Olga stepped from behind a tree trunk and walked towards them. She was carrying a small radio on a strap round her neck. In her other hand she held a revolver. A 9mm Luger. Wartime vintage.

'It makes sense,' Regan said, sorrowfully. 'A man like Seamus O'Brien wouldn't try to run the racket he did in Hamburg without acquiring protection. You were his protection, weren't you, Olga? When he decided to close down his Hamburg operation, he brought you along with him. In the background.'

'We knew there was a leak from the Davidswache,' Ingrid said, as much to Olga as to Regan, 'and they put me on to the job. Olga wasn't very clever at hiding her tracks. Olga, why didn't you come to me? Why didn't you tell me, talk to me . . .?'

Regan heard the note of anguish in Ingrid's voice and suddenly the last part of the jigsaw that had been scrambled when first he met Olga now fell into place. Sure, it's possible to love two people; it's possible to have a deep relationship with two people, a man and a woman. The world's a funny triangulated place and we're only just beginning to find that out, to bring it out into the open.

'Why, Olga, why?' he asked.

Olga smiled, her face twisting with hate. 'You Englishmen,' she said. 'Do you know what year I was born? 1946. Do you know what year Hamburg was liberated? 1945.'

'Your father was an Englishman,' Regan said.

'Very perceptive, Mister Regan, but wrong in only one detail. My father was several Englishmen. A patrol. Finding my mother alone in the rubble of a bombed out Hamburg. Can you wonder it was a pleasure for me to help Seamus O'Brien, to work alongside him to destroy you and all other Englishmen. You were supposed to be in that truck when the radio bomb exploded, *Mister* Regan. You.'

'I knew that part of the story,' Ingrid said. 'About what happened all those years ago. I didn't know about Seamus O'Brien until recently.' She turned to Olga. 'For years, Olga,' she said, 'I stayed in the Davidswache, working undercover in the Reeperbahn, to be near you, to help you, feeling sorry for you after the terrible thing that had happened.'

Olga ran towards her, screeching, pointing the Luger. 'You slut,' she said, 'all the time, pretending, being with me, and yet, when this Englishman turned up going to bed with him.' She stumbled, half fell, but this time, when her hand came up holding the Luger, her finger knuckle was white on the trigger.

Regan ignored regulations, slammed Ingrid sideways and, when the Luger exploded, fired the rifle from the hip. The .303 round took Olga in the chest, stopped her still, pushed her gently over backwards. She fell flat on her back and lay still.

'Come on,' Regan said, 'let's get to hell out of here . . .'

TELEFON

Walter Wager

'It was brilliant,' Strelski insisted as he ground out his cigar. 'Hypnosis. We collected 430 first-class English speakers who'd never been outside the country, drilled them in every detail of American life and then handpicked the cream for drug-assisted hypnosis . . . When we were finished with them, every one of them *really* believed that he or she was the American whose papers he or she carried. We sent them off, and every single one of them got through.'

Now TELEFON, the top-secret book containing the names, phone-numbers and code-phrases of the 150 Russian *sleepers* has been stolen. Someone was activating agents all over America with disastrous effect. These agents had been programmed to prepare the way for World War Three. Their activator had to be stopped . . . by any means, and at whatever cost.

'Fast and furious.'
Sunday Telegraph

'Knock-out entertainment.'
Yorkshire Post

'There are few books that must be read from beginning to end . . . TELEFON surely deserves such recognition. It is a fast-moving, tension-packed thriller with Russian agents on one side and the CIA on the other.'
Express And Star

70 SUTTON PLACE

Joseph DiMona

A searing novel about the private lives of the beautiful people – by the author of LAST MAN AT ARLINGTON.

70 Sutton Place is the most exclusive apartment block in New York – a palace for the very rich and the very famous. People like Pamela Morrow, the film star every man wanted; John MacArthur, the glamorous senator with a roving eye; Madame White, the legendary black blues singer; Harley Widener, the theatre producer; Jay Kohner, the magazine publisher; Bob Taylor, the advertising executive.

But New York is a jungle, and even the very rich can't stay isolated for ever. When both the Mafia and a Black Power group decide to infiltrate the block, the sensuous calm and glitter of 70 Sutton Place is shattered, and its residents find themselves trapped in a web of terror and violence that threatens not only their guilty secrets, but also their lives.

J BARNICOAT
CASH SALES DEPT.,
P.O. BOX 11
FALMOUTH
CORNWALL TR10 9EN

Please send me the following titles

Quantity	SBN	Title	Amount
______			______
______			______
______			______
______			______
______			______
		TOTAL	______

Please enclose a cheque or postal order made out to FUTURA PUBLICATIONS LIMITED for the amount due, including 10p per book to allow for postage and packing. Orders will take about three weeks to reach you and we cannot accept responsibility for orders containing cash.

PLEASE PRINT CLEARLY

NAME ....

ADDRESS ....

....